SYLVIA'S LOT

SYLVIA'S LOT

Teresa Waugh

SINCLAIR-STEVENSON

First published in Great Britain in 1994
by Sinclair-Stevenson
an imprint of Reed Consumer Books Ltd
Michelin House, 81 Fulham Road, London, SW3 6RB
and Auckland, Melbourne, Singapore and Toronto

A CIP catalogue record for this book
is available at the British Library
ISBN 1 85619 419 1

Typeset by CentraCet Ltd, Cambridge
Printed in England by Clays Ltd, St Ives plc

For Simon and Alexandra

I

Sometimes in her loneliness Sylvia would just lie down on the floor beside Prophecy, put her arms round the big shaggy creature and fall peacefully asleep. She had come to love Prophecy with a deep, almost obsessive love which sometimes made her wonder if she really were losing her mind. If Prophecy died she would have to go too. Of that she was sure. Her daughter, Gatey, was old enough now to be able to do without her, and her son and daughter-in-law would hardly notice she had gone.

Both Sylvia's children had silly names derived from different crazes of their father's at the time of their births. Gatey's real name was Pyronia after her father's favourite butterfly, commonly known as 'the Gate-keeper'. Rather more embarrassingly, Evidence was called after an outsider at Lincoln on which his father had won a lot of money the day he was born. Sylvia sometimes wondered how she had countenanced either suggestion, but in those far off days she had felt about Frederick rather as she felt about Prophecy now. She had denied him nothing and to this day, if he turned up at her front door begging for a fiver, she knew she would give it to him if she had it. She would probably give him her last crust of bread. It wasn't that she still loved him, but quite simply that she felt desperately sorry for him and that there was something which she would never cease to find painfully appealing about his face. She certainly didn't miss him and despite her loneliness she would often cast her mind back to those angst-ridden years and sigh gently with relief at the thought that they were over, finished, done with – never to return. It was as if a blinding migraine had lifted, or a nagging back ache been cured. Yes, she might give Frederick her last crust of bread, but she would never take him back to live with her. They had been divorced for five years now, and for the moment she had no idea where he was. A long way away, she hoped. But she didn't really care to dwell on where or on what he was doing. Frederick's prospects were melancholy to contemplate.

Prophecy rolled over on her back and stretched her paws in the air. Sylvia felt cold, she shifted and yawned; the floor was hard. She had been dozing and it must be time to feed the dog. She heaved herself to her feet. Oh dear, she felt so stiff and heavy and old, the spring had long ago gone out of her step. She must try to lose weight and to take a little more exercise. Prophecy could certainly do with more walks, but then everything seemed to be such an effort these days.

'Come on, Prophecy darling,' she said, and added idiotically, 'Din-dins, gnum-gnum, noshy-nosh.'

The dog, who wasn't very young either, got up and stretched again with her hindquarters raised and her paws out in front of her. She shook her huge body, idly wagged her tail and plodded behind Sylvia into the kitchen.

The kitchen was not a very nice room, which was

why Sylvia spent as little time as possible in it. It was poky and small and brown with a high-up, narrow window, the light from which was almost entirely blocked out by a thick laurel hedge only five feet away. She might one day think of redecorating the kitchen, but it would of course be an unnecessary expense and hardly worthwhile if she was likely to be moving on again.

When she came to think about it, the sitting-room wasn't a particularly cheerful room either, with its shabby furnishings and drab cream walls. Its windows looked across a small yard at a garage and a huge oil tank. Sylvia lived in the back of the house, in the old servants' quarters. Not that that worried her. It was warm, she had all the room she needed, it was quiet and private and no one objected to Prophecy. She rather hoped to stay.

After the break-up of her marriage she had gone, taking Gatey with her, to be a live-in housekeeper and companion to a rich old lady, who, after a few years of grumbling and fussing, had taken to her bed and died, leaving Sylvia to look for a new job. By this time Gatey, who had been difficult for years, was more or less grown up, and more or less away from home.

As she opened a tin of dog food, Sylvia felt her bun coming loose and her hair falling down her neck. She quickly fed the dog and glanced at the clock on the wall before going upstairs to tidy her hair and put on some lipstick. It was nearly time to go next door and cook the supper and it was important for her always to look presentable for that. She felt a glow of satisfaction as she brushed her hair and pinned it neatly up. Her thick, red-gold curls had been much admired in her youth and even now, although the colour had faded, they showed no trace of grey.

The kitchen in the main part of the house was large and light with two big windows and an open view across farmland. Two fields away the village church nestled in a fold of the hill, a tall group of beeches beside it. The Rectory had been built at a little distance from the church in about 1830 by a rich incumbent, the scion of a local landed family. Sometimes, in the ten days since she had been here, Sylvia had felt like singing as she crossed from one side of the house to the other – that was only if the front of the house was empty, when it was rather like coming out of a cinema into a bright, sunlit afternoon. It was different if someone was there.

There was no one about and as Sylvia put on an apron and began to busy herself peeling potatoes she started to hum a tune from *La Traviata*, wondering meanwhile whether or not Mr Hardcastle was back from work. Percy to her. But she would never be able to call anyone Percy.

Before coming for her interview she had imagined that Percy Hardcastle would be a small, wizened old man with foxy features and rimless spectacles, a little deaf perhaps, reticent and grumpy . . .

She drove up the drive in her old red Volkswagen which had seen better days and was pleasantly surprised by the agreeable prospect of the Old Rectory. Perhaps Mr Hardcastle would be better than she had dreamed possible, not that in her wildest moments she ever imagined a dashing Mr Rochester or even a quiet, shy gentleman with a penchant for country walks, literature and middle-aged ladies with fading red-gold hair. She was far too wise and old for that, and besides, she wouldn't have wanted the bother.

She stood neatly on the front doorstep with her feet

together, her bag hanging from the crook of her arm, smoothing her gloves over her fingers. She looked down at the black court shoes which she had polished that morning and wondered whether she could afford a new pair, then pulled herself together and firmly rang the bell. The noise of the bell was appallingly shrill and seemed to echo in a hollow house, reinforcing Sylvia's vision of a wizened, foxy little man inside. She waited for what seemed like an eternity before she heard footsteps approaching across the hall. She was feeling nervous and lonely.

How had she come to be standing here, outside this big, strange front door, waiting for an even stranger widower to open it, hoping for a dreary job by which she would be able to keep body and soul together? And why? For no one needed her. She might just as well go and jump off the nearest bridge. How did that golden-haired, hopeful girl of years gone by come to be standing here on this doorstep, begging for such a lonely job? Life's a bugger, she thought angrily as the door was opened.

Percy Hardcastle was a giant of a man, six foot four at least, with a huge belly, a florid face and white, wispy hair. He scowled at Sylvia over his half-moon spectacles, apparently not focusing very well.

For a moment Sylvia thought she recognised that old familiar, bleary-eyed look of a drunk for which she always seemed to be half on the look-out and she felt afraid. She badly needed the job.

'Mrs Sylvia Appleby, I presume?' He spoke in pompous, drawling tones once he had properly focused on her face. He put out his hand to shake hers. 'Do come in, my dear,' he said.

I'm certainly not your dear, she thought crossly. She felt prickly and ill at ease, but she blushed and smiled

5

prettily with her head on one side as she stepped across the threshold.

He ushered her in to a comfortable, lived-in-looking sitting-room and invited her to take a seat. She perched on the edge of an armchair covered in faded William Morris, her bag neatly placed on the floor by her feet, her hands on her knees and her back as straight as a ramrod. He stood in front of her, his back to the fireplace, feet apart, hands clasped loosely behind him, belly thrust forward, shoulders back, head cocked to one side.

'So, Mrs – er – Appleyard,' came the tight-throated drawl, 'you would like to be my housekeeper?' He eyed her coldly up and down. Quite pretty, he thought. A bit dowdy. Probably hasn't had a good screw for God knows how long.

'Could you tell me exactly what the job would entail?' Sylvia asked politely. Inside she was boiling. How dared he look at her like that and presume that she was so desperate to work for him! She should have sat on a higher chair, but it was too late now and anyway it probably wouldn't have made much difference. She wondered what his wife had been like, poor woman.

'I keep a charwoman,' he said, 'but I would require you to shop, attend to the laundry and cook. Can you cook?' he barked.

'Very well indeed,' she replied.

He was surprised by the boldness of her answer and paused a while to discomfort her. 'What you call cooking may well not be what I call cooking,' he eventually said rudely.

'Indeed,' she replied, looking him straight in the eye. Despite her inferior position she was beginning to feel more confident.

'Could you cook a spinach soufflé?' he asked.

'Of course I could. Do you prefer your soufflés *baveux* or well-cooked?'

It was his turn to be disconcerted, and suddenly she felt sorry for him and almost apologised.

'My daughter,' he said, 'is very beautiful. She's a vegetarian. I am not, so when she is here you would be required to cook two separate meals every evening, and twice on Saturdays and Sundays.'

'I don't think that that would present a problem,' Sylvia said gently. She wondered about days off, but she would deal with that later.

'What do you know about cooking for vegetarians?' He leaned forward, stuck his neck out and scowled down at her perched on her chair.

What did she know about cooking for vegetarians? She thought of Gatey. Difficult Gatey. Gatey had been a vegetarian since she was twelve. There was nothing Sylvia didn't know about cooking for vegetarians.

'I will show you around the house,' he said, 'and your accommodation. You would have a separate entrance, which please use. Then we can come back here and discuss the terms. I have some other people to interview within the next few days, but I shall be able to let you know by the middle of next week whether or not you have been selected for the job.'

Sylvia wished she could say that she had other interviews to go to and she wondered if she would be able to cope working for a man like Mr Hardcastle. Perhaps the beautiful daughter would provide a lighter touch.

Hardcastle opened the sitting-room door for her and pompously bowed her through. I know your sort, he thought, you'll be wanting to marry me in no time. Hang your hat up in my hall, move into the front

7

rooms. But you won't succeed. And then he began to think about Jocelyn, perfectly beautiful, virginal Jocelyn.

Two weeks later, with considerable trepidation, Sylvia moved in. Necessity decreed that she accept the job and she had to admit that the pay was not ungenerous.

Sylvia had not yet met Jocelyn, about whom she was beginning to feel quite curious, and as she hummed and put the pan of potatoes on the Aga she was wondering about her – wondering particularly how she had coped with the death of her mother at such an early age. Mrs Hardcastle had died when Jocelyn was ten and now she was twenty-five. So she had been without her mother for over half her life. Of course Sylvia had absolutely no idea what sort of mother Mrs Hardcastle had been, she had only seen the picture of her which stood on the piano in the sitting-room. At least, Sylvia presumed it was of her. It was a dark young woman, slender and smiling, dressed in a wedding dress, leaning on the arm of a young Mr Hardcastle. A Mr Hardcastle without a vast belly, altogether thinner, smoother faced, with thicker, darker hair. Smug, he looked in the picture. Smug and stolid.

Suddenly Sylvia became aware of a presence behind her as she stood adding salt to the potatoes on the Aga. She stopped humming. It was funny the way you could almost always tell when there was someone in the room with you. She turned round to see Mr Hardcastle – Percy – standing there with a glass in his hand. His white hair was tousled in a boyish way and fell forward over his florid face. He was clearly in a genial mood. In the short time that she had been in the job Sylvia had come to know Percy Hardcastle's moods. The rude, bullying tone he had adopted at the interview was not often in evidence. Since she lived next door he had become more cordial, talking loudly at her in an almost flirtatious manner.

'Sylvia Appleyard,' he said. 'A most unusual name. Very English, I imagine. Lincolnshire? Derbyshire?'

'Appleby,' said Sylvia.

'I once knew an Appleyard. Interesting man – he was in the Army with me. Don't know what became of him . . .'

'My name,' said Sylvia, 'is Appleby – Appleby.' She had had enough of this joke – pretence – mistake, whatever it was. Could he really not remember her name?

Percy Hardcastle looked at her. Her cheeks were flushed. Funny, he thought, that she should mind quite so much about her name. Appleyard – Appleby, what was the difference? Sylvia had no business to take herself so seriously. She was not a very interesting woman. Typical of her kind. She should consider herself lucky to have got the job. She'd probably not met many men like him. He wondered what Jocelyn would make of her. He'd told Jocelyn all about Sylvia on the telephone but she hadn't really sounded all that interested. Perhaps she'd seen too many of these bloody women coming and going and was waiting to see if Sylvia would stay before making any comment. He wished Jocelyn would come home. He missed her dreadfully. And loved her. She hadn't been home since Christmas. That was nearly three months ago. Sometimes Hardcastle felt badly hurt by her defection, and sometimes angry. Very angry. Couldn't she see that her father was a lonely old man? Well not that old, but he was nearer seventy than sixty and he had done so much for her, the ungrateful girl. Always put her first, even before her mother died, given her everything she could ever have wanted and more. Above all he had loved her – loved her with a passion. Couldn't she see that he deserved something in return?

'How old's your daughter, then?' he asked Sylvia abruptly, as she laid the table for his supper.

Sylvia had told Hardcastle more than once about Gatey, but he never listened.

'So you've got watercress soup,' she said, 'and there's oxtail keeping warm in the bottom oven, and potatoes. I'll be going now.' And she undid her apron.

Percy Hardcastle didn't want her to go. He wanted someone to talk to while he ate.

'Sit down,' he said, waving a hand towards a chair. 'Have a glass of wine – you don't disapprove of wine do you?'

Sylvia looked straight at him with her pale, sad, blue-grey eyes. 'No,' she said, 'not at all.' Poor man, she thought, I suppose he's lonely too, but she didn't really want to stay.

'I'd love just a small glass,' she said, and sat down.

Hardcastle handed her a glass of white wine and gave himself some more gin. He sat down opposite her at the table and unceremoniously with his arm pushed aside the neat place she had laid for him. He took a gulp from his glass and suddenly Sylvia noticed his eyes going out of focus. He tried to stare at her intently with that terrible drunken look of concentration of a man attempting to appear sober – a horrible look, but one which she knew only too well.

'I,' he said, 'have had a hard life, a very hard life in some ways. You probably wouldn't understand what it is like for a man to bring up a daughter, bring up a daughter on his own – an exceptionally beautiful daughter – a very beautiful daughter indeed – I must tell you about her some time . . .' He began to ramble on incoherently. As hardened drinkers do, he had suddenly gone over the top.

Sylvia wished she was anywhere else but there. She wished he would just tidy up the table and eat his soup and let her go. She wished she had refused the glass of wine. Why did she always manage to surround herself with such impossible, hopeless people, and how on earth, she wondered, could Hardcastle do his work properly and why didn't he retire? She was sure he was past retiring age. She supposed that as head of his own firm of solicitors he must be able to hang around for ever, breathing down everyone else's neck. It couldn't be very good for the firm.

When she had finished her wine and made her get-away back to the safe haven of her own wing and Prophecy, she decided that she would never let that happen again. She had had enough of drunks. And, of course, if it got too impossible she would just have to find another job. She didn't want to do that at the moment. Where was Jocelyn? What help was she?

Hardcastle didn't eat his soup when Sylvia left, despite her admonishments on parting. Instead he got up and staggered into the sitting-room to get some more gin.

'Bloody bitch,' he said to himself as he poured the gin. 'Who does she think she is? The Queen of bloody Sheba!' He turned on the television, it was showing an advertisement for one of the big banks. He couldn't make head or tail of it so he turned it up to maximum volume, but that didn't really help either. He wondered if he might be a bit tight. Couldn't be, after all, he'd hardly had anything to drink.

He slumped onto the sofa, glowered at the television and tried with all his might to make sense of what was going on. 'Nothing but rubbish on the box these days,' he muttered, and fell asleep.

He woke in the small hours, cold and sick. The watercress soup and the oxtail were left uneaten in the kitchen. He couldn't make out what had happened. He couldn't remember anything about the earlier part of the evening as he wound his sad and lonely way to bed.

When Sylvia went to prepare Hardcastle's breakfast the next morning she wasn't entirely surprised to find last night's meal untouched, not that that had ever happened before during the short time she had been at the Old Rectory. Well, the same supper would have to do for tonight. She could hardly waste it.

Back in her own side of the house later in the morning she began again to be swamped by the appalling loneliness of life.

'Prophecy,' she said, 'what are we doing here? When you go, darling, I'll go with you. Don't worry, my love, I'll stick around for you.' She put her arms round the dog's great woolly neck.

She didn't have enough work to fill her time and as yet she knew no one in the neighbourhood. The day stretched ahead, long, grey and empty. She wouldn't even have to do any cooking, what with that oxtail and that soup sitting there.

'Let's find a thriller,' she said to Prophecy. 'I'll take you for a walk later, not that it looks very nice out, but I don't suppose you mind very much about that, do you?'

She found a paperback by Dick Francis. She had no idea whether she had read it before or not. She probably had, but it didn't matter, it would do.

The room darkened and Sylvia was obliged to turn on the light – a gloomy thing to have to do in the middle of the morning. Soon it began to rain and it rained persistently for two or three hours until the yard was awash with water and Sylvia was half way through her thriller.

'I've no idea,' as usual she addressed Prophecy, 'whether I've read this book before or not. It seems familiar but I really can't remember who did it. When do you think Gatey will come and see us then? She might be a little curious about where we are.' She put down the book and stared out at the rain in the yard. 'Not much chance of a walk today,' she said. 'If you're lucky, you'll get a run round the house and that'll be it. I wish Gatey would come.'

She didn't think about Evidence coming. There was very little chance indeed of that. In fact, she could hardly remember when she had last seen her son. He'd never been one to keep very much in touch.

Evidence, meanwhile, was nursing a cold in bed in his new house on a new estate in Manchester.

His wife brought him a cup of tea and stirred the sugar in it for him. 'Do you think we ought to do something about your mother?' she asked.

'What for?' Evidence replied crossly. He blew his nose loudly. His eyes were streaming and he had a headache. Milly ought to know better than to start talking about his mother at a time like this. He had a dreadful cold to contend with. 'If she needs us she knows where we are, she can always get in touch,' he said.

'I was just thinking that she may be rather lonely in her new place. Perhaps you might give her a ring.'

'Not when I'm feeling like this,' said Evidence. 'She'll be perfectly all right. She's got a good job by the sound of it, somewhere to live, nothing to complain about. Gatey'll probably go and see her some time.'

Milly sighed. Evidence was sometimes rather selfish.

★

The day after the night before, Percy Hardcastle arrived at work with a niggling feeling of discomfort which he was unable to relate to anything specific. It was almost like a tiny worm of guilt. But guilt about what? He was a very decent fellow who was unlikely to have done anything wrong. Certainly nothing to dwell on. Yesterday evening had been perfectly pleasant. He'd had a good supper – he couldn't remember what it had been – but that woman was definitely quite a decent cook. To drown his feelings of discomfort, he adopted an especially bonhomous air, patted all the men in the office on the shoulder and, to their annoyance, called the women 'my dear'.

II

Lady Field was working herself up into one of her regular fevers of resentment against the world. There was she, living all alone and not one of them giving a damn for her after all she had done for everyone else. She had never been a selfish person and what thanks did she ever get from any single member of her family for all the effort and self-sacrifice of years – for the love and devotion? Of course they didn't realise what she had been through for them. No imagination, that was their trouble. She picked up the telephone and dialled her neighbour's number.

'Ah, Cynthia,' she began, 'I'm all alone – not that there's anything new about that – and I can't get out, I really feel too under the weather. I need a few things from the shops, you might like to pop out for me, it'd probably do you good to get out and I expect you'd be pleased to get away from the family for half an hour, although I'm sure your family are more considerate than mine. They never come to see me – none of them. The trouble is that I suppose I've spoilt them all, been far too good to them, so that now all they can do is to think about themselves. It's all my own fault I suppose, and of course my daughter is very selfish, she's taken quite after her father, very self-absorbed and hard, quite hard you know . . .'

Cynthia couldn't get a word in edgeways. She just allowed the angry stream of consciousness to flow, there was nothing else she could do. Of course she never minded doing the occasional bit of shopping for the old lady, in fact she didn't really mind the vitriol flowing like lava down the telephone as long as she had the time and was feeling strong enough for it. Lady Field was an interesting character study and an object lesson in how not to alienate one's own children.

As soon as she had put the telephone down, Lady Field marched angrily into the kitchen to look for inspiration — she would have to find something she needed from the shops. She opened the cupboards but they all seemed well-stocked. She had plenty of marmalade, mustard, tea, coffee, salt, pepper. She'd better think of something she needed, that wretched woman would be round in a minute. She was a very tiresome woman, Cynthia. Lady Field didn't want her coming in and expecting cups of tea. She had better have her shopping list ready to give the woman as soon as she got to the front door. Cynthia was the sort of woman who would be prepared to sit in your kitchen for hours, just getting under your feet.

Lady Field found a pad of paper and wrote neatly at the top of the first sheet: 'Lady Field's shopping list'. She underlined it twice and then wondered what to write next. She had enough bread, but then she could always freeze an extra loaf. It would never do to run out of bread. So she wrote '1) Bread' and then paused for thought. '2) Button mushrooms', she wrote next for no very good reason at all.

The front door bell rang and Lady Field went to open it to find Cynthia smiling on the doorstep.

'Oh, Cynthia,' she said, 'you really are a dear. So very kind. Now come in and sit down for a minute while I make my list.'

'I mustn't be long,' Cynthia said, looking at her watch, 'I have to get back in time to take the twins to their ballet class.'

'Of course you all spoil your children so much these days,' Lady Field retorted with a snort. 'Now sit down, dear, while I make you a cup of tea.'

'Well just a quick one – that would be very kind,' Cynthia said apprehensively.

Half an hour later Cynthia was trying desperately to go.

'Now, I've put bread,' Lady Field was saying, 'and I don't mind if it's white or brown. I don't want it sliced, I don't care for sliced bread, but I like those round, brown, granary loaves – you know the ones, dear? So, bread – brown bread – or white if you can find one of those nice, crusty cottage loaves, but on the whole I think I prefer brown. Well, get anything you like, I don't care, I shall be dead soon . . .'

Cynthia thought she would never get away, but she eventually did, after another ten minutes. She wondered how long it would take to drop the shopping back.

As she shut the front door behind Cynthia, Lady Field felt the velvet touch of her black cat rubbing past her leg.

'Blast!' she said aloud and quite angrily. 'I've forgotten you, Puss.'

It was too late to call Cynthia back and of course the poor girl was so busy, what with the twins' ballet lessons and so forth, so she would hardly have time to go out again for cat food when she got back. Lady Field wondered how on earth Cynthia managed to do all the things she had to do. The young these days were quite amazing. But she would have to find someone who could go and get the cat food for her. She'd ring Milly. It was high time that Milly thought of someone other than herself – herself or Evidence. In Lady Field's opinion Milly spoilt her husband, mind you, she was obviously besotted with the man, and you could see why. No one could deny that Evidence was good-looking.

Milly was very angry. As much with herself as with Lady Field. It would probably take her an hour to cross the whole of Manchester and then it would take even longer to get back. She couldn't think why she had agreed to go out and buy that ridiculous cat food! Surely there was someone nearer who could have been called upon? In fact, Milly wondered why on earth Lady Field couldn't go out and get it for herself. It was only a seven minute walk to the shop from Lady Field's house. If that. Besides, it would no doubt do her the world of good to get out and take herself for a walk. Give her something to do.

'Why the hell did you agree?' Evidence shouted angrily from his bed, where he was still nursing his cold. 'She's a selfish old bag. Tell her to get it herself.'

Milly had often noticed that Evidence really disliked her ever doing a good turn for anyone other than himself, which annoyed her and so she suddenly felt better disposed to spending a whole afternoon in search of a tin of cat food.

'My granddaughter-in-law, Milly, is a wonderful girl,' Lady Field was telling the window-cleaner in her kitchen over a cup of tea. 'She'll do anything for me – and she's such a pretty girl, and a nurse. She's working nights at the moment. I don't know how she does it. It must be a dreadful strain. And then in the daytime she has to look after her husband and her house. Her husband's a very demanding man – quite selfish. Just like all men,' she added archly. 'But to tell you the truth I think she really ought to insist on lying down and having a proper rest in the day. She'll wear herself out. She ought to be able to say no to her husband sometimes.'

Milly delivered the cat food and spent half an hour or so chatting to Lady Field before going home again.

Lady Field had a great deal of advice to offer Milly on the subject of how to deal with her husband. She had never pandered to her husband or spoilt him, she would certainly never have waited on him in bed with a cold. She had never heard such nonsense. Once you started on that path, there was no turning back. 'Stand up to them and make sure you have things your way from the start!' was her advice to Milly.

Milly had heard it all before, but she listened again, quietly amused. After all, Lady Field must have gone wrong somewhere since Sir Kenneth – knighted for his services to local government – had, at the last ditch, left a lifetime of servitude to the Draconian rule of his wife and settled in France with a Belgian divorcée, where he had subsequently died, leaving everything he owned to the Belgian lady in question. Some people considered Lady Field's adoption of the title 'Lady' as rather droll, since her husband was not knighted until two months after the decree nisi. But no one ever dared refer to the discrepancy. Lady Field herself had long since forgotten the sequence of events and had she been challenged she would have sworn – and believed herself to be telling the truth – that he had been knighted several years before the divorce. She could even remember going to Buckingham Palace. The Queen, who was so gracious, had been dressed in a beautiful shade of buttercup yellow. The Queen always looked well in yellow.

For some reason which she couldn't really understand, Milly had a soft spot for Lady Field. She could see that her behaviour was preposterous, but not being directly related to the old lady she felt somewhat detached and therefore able to admire her for her sheer guts and determination.

After Milly had gone Lady Field fussed around the kitchen for a while, looking for a tin-opener. If she couldn't find a tin-opener there would be very little point to the tin of cat food. Sometimes she thought she really must be getting Alzheimer's. She was growing so forgetful these days. Eventually she found the tin-opener in her hand, where it had been for at least five minutes.

'All's well then, Puss,' she said, 'you can have some supper after all.' Then she went on to tell the cat all about Milly and what a wonderful girl she was, but how very badly she organised her life. 'I mean, imagine coming all this way just to deliver a tin of cat food. The girl must be out of her mind. After all, I could perfectly well have walked round to the shops myself. It would have made a little outing, wouldn't it, Puss?'

Later that evening, after having worked herself into a further fever of impotent rage, Lady Field decided to telephone her daughter. There was no point in waiting for Sylvia to telephone her, she might have to wait for six months. Of course, Sylvia couldn't possibly imagine what it was like to be old and alone. It was all right for her, she had a good job and children who took trouble over her.

'Hallo, darling,' she began, in a faint, trembly voice. 'I'm sorry if I'm being a bore, but I just had to talk to someone. I haven't spoken to a soul for three days.'

'Oh, Mummy, I'm so sorry, what's the matter with you?' Sylvia replied, genuinely anxious despite the multitude of times her mother had shot the same line before.

'I'm not at all well,' Lady Field's voice was even fainter than at first. 'I think I'm going to have to go to hospital. Well they don't know at all what the matter is, but I shall have to have tests . . .'

'What tests Mummy?'

'I don't know what tests – just tests,' Lady Field tried to make the tests sound as mysterious and as threatening as possible.

Sylvia was worried, partly because she realised that it might be her abominable duty to go and nurse her mother and partly because, whatever the circumstances, she was loath to go away so soon after starting her new job.

'By the way,' Lady Field suddenly veered right into a different mode, 'Milly came to see me today . . .'

'I thought you said you hadn't seen anyone for three days?'

'Well, Milly doesn't count and anyway she only put her head around the door for two minutes. You know what she's like – too busy ever to stop and think about anyone else. Of course I suppose Evidence just married his mother all over again. They say that that's what some men do. Well, it would be bound to suit Evidence, wouldn't it? First of all you spoilt him to death, and now that silly girl is spoiling him.'

Sylvia began to feel a surge of anger welling up inside her, but, even after all these years, she had no idea how to protect herself from it, or how to parry the attack.

'So when do you think you will have to go to hospital?' she asked.

21

'Hospital? What are you talking about hospital for? I'm not going to hospital.'

'But I thought you said something about tests.'

'Tests, yes, but I don't think I'll have them, they won't be necessary, I'm perfectly all right – well, I expect I'll be all right,' she added faintly, returning to her earlier, frailer mode.

Sylvia sighed inwardly with relief; she had been let off the hook again.

'Perhaps you would like to come and stay for a few days and see where I am. It's very pretty around here and I could take you to the sea.'

'To the sea! It's hardly the time of year to go to the sea. What on earth would I want to go to the sea for?'

'Well do at least come and stay, I'd love you to come,' Sylvia urged.

'No you wouldn't, you don't want me at all,' her mother snapped.

'Of course I do, you know I do, please come,' Sylvia sounded almost childish. She always hated herself when she adopted that silly childish tone with her mother, but she did it now because she was feeling guilty – guilty at her relief. Relief not that there was nothing the matter with Lady Field, so much as at the knowledge that she needn't – not yet at least – go to Manchester and nurse her. If it did ever come to that she wondered if she would be able to get away with staying with Evidence and Milly. The trouble was that Evidence and Milly were rather far away and she supposed that half the point would be the fact of being with her mother overnight. Sylvia had a total horror of ever staying the night in her mother's house. She could not envisage any situation from which she would rather escape.

'If you really insist then, darling, I'll come down for a couple of weeks or so in April. That'll give me something to look forward to.' And so the conversation ended on an amicable tone, leaving Lady Field delighted and Sylvia somewhat apprehensive.

The very next day Lady Field was feeling in a much better and brighter frame of mind. For one thing she was genuinely quite pleased at the prospect of a trip south to see her daughter. She even thought it might be quite nice to go on an outing to the sea after all. She told her cleaning lady that her daughter had rung and invited her. Sylvia, she said, was quite an admirable person in many ways, very hard-working and most intelligent. 'I can't imagine where she inherited her intelligence from,' she added with a smirk. Sir Kenneth hadn't had a brain in his head – that was made quite clear by his choice of the Belgian divorcée. She thought of ringing Milly to tell her of her planned visit, but decided against it. She didn't want Milly to start thinking that she was all right and that there was no need to bother to look in. It was important to keep Milly on her toes.

Later, she did ring Milly, but only to complain about Cynthia, who was such a stupid woman that you couldn't even trust her to buy a loaf of bread for you. No, she herself was perfectly all right, there was no need for Milly to do anything, but it would be lovely to see her some time. At the weekend perhaps. The weekends were always so long and lonely when you lived on your own.

Bearing that in mind, Milly rang her mother-in-law at the weekend. She did wish Evidence would take more trouble about his mother. He bore her no grudge as far as she could see, so she could never really understand why it was that he seemed so loath to do anything about her.

In fact Evidence had such horrible memories of his

23

childhood that he wished to cut himself off from it completely, even if it meant losing contact with his mother for whom, if he thought about it, he felt sorry, and about whom he felt guilty. It was better then not to think about her. He wished Milly hadn't such a soft heart and weren't so very dutiful, or that if she were she would confine it to her own family.

Sylvia was delighted to hear from Milly, although she sometimes felt a pang of disappointment that it was never her son who rang. Milly told her about Lady Field and the cat food and they both laughed. Sylvia told Milly about her mother possibly having to go to hospital.

'I'm sure that's not true,' said Milly. 'She was in fine fettle when I saw her and she certainly never said anything about hospital to me.'

Sylvia was reassured. She could never be absolutely certain whether or not her mother was bluffing.

On Sunday afternoon Milly needed to get out of the house. Evidence's cold had left him very short tempered and he wanted to catch up on some paperwork. She decided to leave him to it and to take herself for a walk in the park. It was a lovely day and spring was in the air at last. The municipal daffodils were all bursting into bloom and the public gardens were bright with crocuses.

Milly had been brought up in Manchester and she wouldn't live anywhere else in the world for preference. In fact, it was she who had urged Evidence to come and settle there. They had met while they were both working in London and they had lived together there for nearly three years before getting married and moving back to Manchester. Even then they had to wait for him to be able to find the right job in computers. At first there had been the added problem of Lady Field. Evidence was not at all sure that he was prepared to live in the same city as his grandmother, but he eventually agreed on condition that they lived right on the other side of the town and on condition that he never had to see her. The second condition was ridiculous, but Milly just shrugged her shoulders and agreed. It was nothing to her whether or not her husband saw his grandmother and Milly was dying to get back to Manchester and to her own warm and loving family.

Milly sat on a park bench and gazed at a show of daffodils. She and Evidence had moved back in November and at times throughout the grisly, wet, northern winter Milly had been at pains to convince him that they had done the right thing. Spring would come, she assured him, even to Manchester. She wished he was beside her now to witness those daffodils trumpeting forth their promise. Daffodils, she thought, were always triumphant. A squirrel ran up a tree, with a black and white spaniel in hot pursuit, two boys skateboarded past and an old tramp came shuffling along the path, mumbling into his long, grey beard, his hands thrust deep into the pockets of a huge, shabby, tweed overcoat. All seemed right with the world to Milly. The tramp, she fantasised, was probably quite happy with the way of life he had chosen, free from the ordinary troubles of the daily round. As he drew near he noticed her looking at him and he stopped and nodded.

'A lovely day,' said Milly.

'Indeed,' said the tramp and hesitated an instant before suggesting that he sit for a moment beside her.

Milly was in an open, friendly mood. 'Of course, sit down,' she said. 'It's not my personal bench, you know,' and she laughed whilst moving herself to the very edge of the bench, leaving plenty of space for the tramp to spread himself over.

He sat down at a polite distance from Milly, but not far enough away for her not to catch a great gust of BO, tobacco, alcohol, sweat and dirt of every kind.

'I was just admiring the daffodils. Aren't they lovely?' Milly said. 'I always love it when the daffodils come out. The only trouble is that they never seem to last very long. I sometimes think they're my favourite flowers.'

'"Fair daffodils,"' said the tramp, '". . . We have short time to stay, as you, We have as short a spring; As quick a growth to meet decay . . ."'

'Pardon?' said Milly.

'Don't they teach you any poetry at school these days?' the tramp asked.

'Well, I left school several years ago,' said Milly. 'But no, we didn't really do poetry. Sometimes we had to write it though.'

'I'm so sorry,' said the tramp, 'you look so very young, I thought you must be a schoolgirl.'

'No,' Milly giggled, 'I'm a nurse.' And she added hurriedly, 'I'm married.'

'Married!' the tramp gave a hollow laugh. 'You certainly look too young for that. "Then be not coy, but use your time; And while ye may go marry . . ."' The tramp laughed again.

Milly was beginning to feel a little uncomfortable. This man was very odd.

'Marriage is a peculiar thing indeed,' he went on, 'an unobtainable condition of course. Something to be aspired to by some of us perhaps, but not necessarily to be enjoyed. Certainly not enjoyed. Can prison be enjoyed?' "But let me not to the marriage of true minds admit impediment . . ."'

Milly hadn't the faintest idea what the man was going on about. Suddenly she felt as though he had somehow cast a blight over this lovely spring day.

'Well I think I ought to be getting back now,' she said, standing up. 'Goodbye.'

'It's a shame they don't teach you any proper poetry at school these days,' the tramp said gently.

Milly walked away, glad to have escaped and to be back in her familiar everyday world, but when she had gone a little way she could not resist a look round over her shoulder to where the tramp was sitting on the bench. She saw him pull a bottle out of his pocket and take a great swig. Poor fellow, she thought. A nut case. And she walked on.

The tramp spent that night on the park bench. He considered himself quite lucky to get away with it and not to have been moved on by the police, or worse still, to have been beaten up by gangs of louts. When he woke in the morning he was cold and stiff and it was only just getting light. He looked at the daffodils which the girl had so admired, glowing in the half light. ' "We have short time to stay, as you," ' he said out loud to them. ' "We have as short a spring; As quick a growth to meet decay . . ." ' Occasionally it occurred to him to wonder if that was true. To him man's allotted span sometimes seemed to last for eternity. He looked around; there didn't seem to be anyone about so he took a leak against what looked like a laburnum tree.

He needed a cup of tea badly. He still had a few pence in his pocket for that. It was just a question of finding a café open, but he thought he knew which way to go. He pulled his bottle out of his pocket and squinted at it. There was half an inch of liquor left. He knocked it back in one go.

'Bagh!' he said, and then, 'Lord have mercy, Christ have mercy!'

That Monday afternoon Lady Field was shopping in the Arndale centre. She was fed up with the four walls of her house and had persuaded another neighbour, a Mrs Curtis, to take her shopping. Mrs Curtis was a dull woman and a very dangerous driver – Lady Field wondered she dared travel with her, but the woman had nothing else to do so she might as well make herself useful. In fact Mrs Curtis worked full time, and had just got a few days off; her husband, who had recently been made redundant, was at home coping with a mother-in-law with Alzheimer's and a retarded teenage son. To Lady Field a redundant husband meant a wife who could be entirely at her disposal.

The two women were just coming out of W.H. Smith, having been shopping for quite long enough, when they very nearly bumped into a tramp with a long, grey beard, his hands thrust deep into the pockets of a hugh, shabby, tweed coat.

'Poor fellow,' said Mrs Curtis. 'It makes you wonder when you see someone like that – I mean, how did he get into that condition?'

'In my opinion,' said Lady Field, 'people like that should be cleared off the streets . . .' But as she spoke she froze. She put out her hand and clasped Mrs Curtis round the wrist to prevent herself from falling. She turned round and the tramp turned round at the same time. Their eyes met.

'What's the matter, dear, are you all right?' Mrs Curtis sounded concerned.

'The bitch,' muttered the tramp to himself. 'Christ have mercy. Lord have mercy.'

'It was just a little turn,' said Lady Field. 'Nothing at

all really, I just felt a little dizzy. I expect I'm tired from shopping and all the crowds.'

'We'll get home as quick as we can now and I'll make you a nice cup of tea,' Mrs Curtis said kindly.

Lady Field had recovered herself. The adrenalin was flowing. 'Well don't drive too fast, will you dear. I don't want to end up in the casualty ward. You're quite terrifying to drive with, even when you're not in a hurry.'

When Mrs Curtis dropped her home she refused to allow her to come in – she was quite all right and she could perfectly well make her own tea, she just wanted the woman out of the way. She needed to be alone for a while to think. What, she wondered, was she going to do with her newly acquired information? How could it best be used and to what ends? Of one thing she was certain – she had better sleep on it.

III

There were usually five people living in Gatey's squat.
But as often as not there were a few extra when you
woke up on any given morning. Gatey had been in
Hackney for over a year and although she still thoroughly believed in the principle of squatting, she had
begun to go away rather more often for weekends or
the odd night. She didn't really like to admit it, even to
herself, but she did miss the occasional hot bath.
Besides, the derelict house smelt unpleasantly of damp.

When she went away for weekends though, it was
not usually to stay with her mother, so much as with
friends' parents, or even her brother in Manchester. It
was not that she didn't love her mother. She loved her
very much indeed. But the trouble was that she and her
mother simply could not see eye to eye, so that every
meeting between them ended in a terrific row and tears.
Gatey wished desperately that her mother could understand that it was perfectly reasonable for her to live off
the dole and that squatting, far from being wrong – or
stealing as Sylvia would have it – was both morally
desirable and socially useful.

Sylvia, on the other hand, knew that Gatey was

basically a moral person, that a lot of 'properly brought-up' young people these days thought as Gatey did, and she was even prepared to listen to Gatey's arguments in favour of squatting. And in the end it was not that she could really fault the arguments, but that she quite simply could not bear Gatey to be doing it. Old habits and old attitudes die hard and Sylvia had not been brought up to think that living on the dole, or squatting, was something that any right-minded person would ever dream of doing out of choice. It smelt of decadence to her, and of the 'grab-have' generation. And yet there was absolutely nothing 'grab-have' about Gatey. She had other problems, but never that.

Another thing that worried Sylvia about Gatey's attitude was that, if you looked at it in a certain light, it bore a niggling resemblance to much of what had been her father's way of thinking. And it hadn't done him any good. Besides, if she went on for long like this, would she ever get a home of her own? One thing to be said for Evidence was that he appeared to be settled. Sylvia didn't really feel that she had to worry about him, especially now he had lovely Milly to look after him. She only hoped that he looked after Milly, too. Sylvia had worked all her life to provide a sensible, stable home for herself and her children and everything always seemed to have gone wrong. She didn't mean to complain, things could be a great deal worse and, anyway, some people were always bound to be luckier than others. It was just that she would love to see Gatey with more security than she herself seemed to have had, and less of a battle to fight.

A further source of irritation between Gatey and her mother centred on Gatey's hair. Gatey could never understand why it was that people's parents seemed to mind so much about what they did to their hair and

Sylvia herself wondered why it was that she minded so much; after all, it would grow again. Gatey had inherited her mother's thick, red-gold curls which lately she had taken to shaving off very, very close to her head indeed, leaving her slightly sticking-out ears, adorned with half a dozen earrings each, fully exposed. Sylvia just felt irritated whenever she looked at her daughter. And Gatey sensed the irritation, which she regarded as quite irrational.

Despite all these differences Gatey wished she saw her mother a little more often. Sylvia was the only person on whom Gatey had ever felt that she could truly rely. At the moment she had a really unreliable boyfriend to whom she was vaguely thinking of giving the push. But every time she thought of coming to the point, he looked rather hopeless and appealing and she felt sorry for him and postponed the decision to a later date. Perhaps it would be a good thing to get away from him for a while so as to harden her heart against the deed.

With this in mind she proposed herself to stay for a few days with her mother. Two or three days were the most she could cope with. In fact what she did was to hitch a lift to Tunbridge Wells and then ring Sylvia.

'Hi, Mum,' she said, 'it's me. I'm in Tunbridge Wells, can you come to get me?'

Gatey had been wrong to suppose that Tunbridge Wells was her mother's nearest town. She should have gone to Battle. She was also very lucky to find her mother at home. Sylvia had just shut the front door behind her and was about to go out shopping for the afternoon. For a moment she thought she would leave the telephone to ring, but changed her mind and dashed back in to catch it just in time.

Despite her delight in seeing her daughter, Sylvia felt

that things had got off to a bad start. Perhaps her annoyance at the short hair and rows of earrings was still somehow insufficiently concealed, or perhaps it was Gatey having hitchhiked with only a plastic bag for luggage which ruffled Sylvia's feathers. Gatey was of the opinion that just because men were such uncontrollable beasts as to roam the country raping and molesting women whenever they felt the urge, there was no reason why she should have her liberties curtailed. She had as much right to hitch or to walk the streets at night as anyone else in the land.

Sylvia wondered if she would apply the same logic to lions in the African bush or tigers in the Indian jungle. Gatey pointed out that tigers in the Indian jungle did not wantonly eat humans. Sylvia, on the other hand, had seen a fascinating television programme about a man-eating tiger in a village in northern India. And so the argument continued with neither Gatey nor her mother really remembering what had provoked it and with aggression and intolerance mounting on both sides so that they both became more and more unhappy whilst inwardly longing for harmony and yet incapable of taking the first step to establish it.

Eventually the argument petered out and the conversation was reduced to icy politeness, with Gatey enquiring about Prophecy's well-being and Sylvia replying brightly, but coldly. Sylvia adored Prophecy but she knew quite well that Gatey didn't, and she had no desire to discuss her beloved with a mocking onlooker.

They drove all the way back to Battle, where Sylvia was just in time to do her shopping, and then home to be greeted so ecstatically by Prophecy that even Gatey's heart melted.

Harmony was then restored and Gatey's attention turned to looking around her mother's new home and

33

questioning her in detail about Mr Hardcastle. She rather wished her mother would remarry; she must be lonely, with a somewhat bleak future looming ahead and very little excitement in store, just endless drudgery. She thought her mother was still jolly pretty. She just wished she would make a bit more of an effort and not look so apologetic all the time. She also realised that if Sylvia remarried, the pressure would be off her. She did worry about her mother and feel sad for her, but she couldn't come and see her all the time, after all, she had her own life to be getting on with. Besides, Evidence did very little to help.

'So how old is he?' Gatey wanted to know.

'I don't know. Sixty-six, sixty-seven, something like that I should think.'

'Oh, ancient,' Gatey remarked. 'But what's he look like? Is he handsome?'

'Rather red-faced and a bit on the fat side, if you call that handsome.' Sylvia knew exactly what Gatey was getting at.

'And do you like him, Mum?' Gatey was insistent.

'I don't really know him very well. After all, I do most of the work when he's out of the house during the day.' Sylvia was always able to avoid the issue when she wanted to. In fact she had taken to doing her very best to see as little as possible of Percy Hardcastle since she found his drunken confidences and heavy-handed flattery even more difficult to bear than his moods of overweening pomposity and boorish ill-manners.

'I'm dying to see him,' said Gatey, and then: 'Don't think much of your view. Don't you get depressed looking out at that dreary old yard? Couldn't you put some flower pots in it or something, just to brighten it up?'

Sylvia felt touchy, she knew that Gatey was trying to

34

be kind, but Gatey didn't really understand. How could she? 'There's hardly enough light for flowers there,' she said, 'and besides, the yard does not belong to me.'

Gatey looked at her mother and suddenly realised what a very sad face she had. She crossed the room and put her arm around her. 'Cheer up, Mum,' she said. 'We'll all be dead in a hundred years or something.'

Sylvia smiled, but she felt like crying. She always did when people were nice to her.

When Gatey did meet Percy Hardcastle she was absolutely furious. She was in his kitchen with her mother, helping her prepare some vegetables for his supper, when he came in to see what was going on, and probably in search of company. His mood was one of brash over-familiarity mixed with conceit: no one, he said, could cook vegetables like he could; his mange-touts were a poem. He kissed his finger tips and threw the kiss into the air. Brussels sprouts were among his favourites and he could explain why it was that so many people disliked them – it was because English people never failed to overcook them. Brussels sprouts needed to be tiny and they should only be cooked in fast boiling water for the briefest of moments.

'You aren't proposing, I trust,' he said, pointing to the vegetables which Sylvia was preparing, 'to drown those in water and cook them until they are grey. What you should do with those . . .'

'If you're so good at cooking, why don't you cook them yourself? Mum could have a rest,' Gatey said, staring him straight in the face.

Sylvia was half proud of Gatey and half ashamed of her. How, she asked herself, had she managed to bring her daughter up to be so rude? There was no doubt that Gatey was both outspoken and bold but she was rude, too, and Sylvia was ashamed of that and felt responsible for it.

'Gatey,' she said, 'please . . .' and to Percy Hardcastle, 'I'm sorry, I really am sorry, I am so sorry . . .'

All this apologising gave rise to another quarrel with Gatey when they later returned to Sylvia's side of the house. They were sitting in the poky kitchen, having a cup of coffee before going to bed.

'I can't think how you put up with him, Mum,' Gatey said. 'He's a complete pig and I hate the way he treats you, and anyway I don't want you to apologise for me. You may not be prepared to say anything, but I just don't see why he should get away with it.'

Sylvia tried to explain to her daughter, as she had done a thousand times before, that there were some things you couldn't change and those were the things which you just had to learn to tolerate. There was no point whatsoever in her picking a quarrel with Mr Hardcastle because the job was a good one for her and she needed it.

Gatey was young and if she believed in anything she believed in the perfectability of society, in fighting for what she believed in, in not allowing herself to be trampled on. Neither should her mother allow herself to be trampled on.

'I can't see why you think this is such a wonderful job,' she said with feeling. 'It's a rubbishy job – working for a revolting, great fat drunk who was probably a wife beater; he's rude to you and he talks down to you – he's the worst kind of old-fashioned male and a filthy lecher – didn't you notice the way he looked at my tits?'

'Oh Gatey, please . . .' Sylvia winced. 'I hate the language you use.'

Gatey just went straight on. 'Well, it's true, he's revolting and it isn't even as if you've got anywhere nice to live!' She waved her arms around. 'Just look at this place, it's so gloomy and drab – it's just like a school.'

Sylvia buried her face in her hands. She wanted to cry but she could not bear to cry in front of Gatey.

And Gatey could not bear what she saw as weakness in her mother. 'Chuck it in,' she said. 'Go out there and look for another job – one with decent people, get somewhere nice to live . . .'

Sylvia thought of the squat in Hackney which she had visited a couple of times and smiled. 'One man's meat,' she said wryly, 'is another man's poison.'

'But this place would be anybody's poison.'

'I'm sorry, darling, I hate to upset you, but I don't want to go haring around looking for new jobs all the time and I'm perfectly all right here really. I'm just sorry that you should be so upset.'

'Please don't keep apologising!' Gatey was almost screaming. She could see that her mother was upset, too, but she herself would never apologise. She had watched her mother saying sorry for as long as she could remember: to Lady Field, to her father when he was blind drunk, to Evidence, to Mr Hardcastle, to everybody, and she had observed that it was a mistake. Apart from anything else, her mother had absolutely nothing to apologise about. Gatey looked at her and realised that she was on the verge of tears and that it was partly her own fault for shouting at her, but still she would not say she was sorry. Saying sorry was negative – look where it had got Sylvia. Precisely nowhere, in Gatey's opinion.

'Don't cry, Mum,' she said gently, 'and don't give in. Don't let them grind you down; people have been grinding you down all your life.'

Sylvia knew that what her daughter said was true, in

a way, but she also knew that she was beginning to run out of steam for the fight and that her natural desire for peace and quiet would always win the day in the end, even if it meant putting up with what other people might regard as intolerable conditions. Her main complaint, where the present situation was concerned, was loneliness. She had no need to see very much of Percy Hardcastle and she was perfectly happy with her lodgings, which could be brightened up with a lick of paint here and there, but she did hope very much indeed that somehow she would find a small circle of friends, or at least acquaintances, sooner or later. But she was very much aware that she had always found making friends difficult because of an in-built conviction that whenever she approached other people, she was intruding on them.

There was no point at Sylvia's age in blaming her mother for the past. Lady Field was as she was and she would never change now, but it was strange how often Sylvia could hear the echo of her mother's tones ringing in her ears.

'Just remember, dear, that no one is interested in what you have to say.' And, 'You have had no experience of life, so don't try to push yourself forward, dear,' and, 'If you were a pretty girl, that would be different, dear.' Always that dreadful 'dear'. Sylvia sometimes wondered if she hated her mother, but, no, of course she didn't. Poor Lady Field was lonely too, which of course was why she made herself so difficult.

Gatey didn't agree with any of that. She saw her grandmother as a wicked old witch who had ruined her mother's life. She was perfectly furious when she heard that Lady Field was on her way to see Sylvia and that she planned to spend nearly a fortnight staying with her.

'You must be mad!' she said. 'I couldn't put up with that old bag for more than twenty-four hours – if that. Anyway, she has a dreadful effect on you, you become all tense when she's around for just five minutes.' Gatey had even seen her mother's hand shaking before having to telephone Lady Field. 'If you were as jealous of me as she is of you, and as foul to me as she is to you, I wouldn't bother to come and see you ever,' Gatey continued her attack.

They had discussed this so many times before and Sylvia always took the line that she owed her mother something and that it was her duty to be as nice to her as she could, although it was sometimes hard. But she did draw comfort from Gatey's violent championing of her own side, was glad that Gatey could talk to her as she, in a lifetime, would never address her mother and even felt a secret burst of pleasure at hearing Lady Field described, so unequivocally and with such disdain, as an old bag.

'Tell her she can't come for that long,' Gatey went on. 'Tell her you haven't got room – that I'm coming, that you're going away, that she just can't come. Tell her to bugger off . . .'

Sylvia wondered what on earth would happen if she did one day just turn round and tell her mother to bugger off. It was unimaginable. She could count on the fingers of one hand the number of times she had stood up to her mother, even in the mildest of ways.

Sometimes Gatey reminded Sylvia of Frederick, who always used to urge her to stand up to her mother. 'Keep that dreadful mother of yours away from me!' he used to say. Not very Christian, Sylvia thought. Certainly not how a clergyman ought to talk.

'Pity you and Dad ever split up,' Gatey said as though

reading her mother's thoughts. 'He'd have kept her at bay.'

'No, Gatey, don't say that.' Gatey was stepping on dangerous ground. 'And don't romanticise your father. He had his good points, but you know it was impossible.' Sylvia loathed talking about Frederick to her children. In fact she loathed talking about him to anybody. Somehow it was all still too painful.

When she was married to him – especially towards the end – she could only see the drunken, aggressive bully, hell-bent on self-destruction and then the man with a hangover and shaking hands, full of self-loathing, abject and grovelling for forgiveness, swearing he would never touch another drop of liquor. In those days she had been afraid for him and for herself; all her energies had gone to protecting the children and covering up for Frederick in the parish. Life had been hell and Frederick had been a monster. Since separating from him a different, strange, distant picture had developed. It was not as if she called this picture to mind on purpose, but it just presented itself to her. In it she saw two men standing side by side, silently. They were both Frederick. The one on the left-hand side as she looked at them was always Frederick as she had known him at first: tall, good-looking, debonair, attractive, humorous. The one on the right was the other Frederick: scowling, angry, unsteady on his feet, a glass in his hand, bleary-eyed, a dark, brooding, unhappy, resentful man. Was it all her fault, she wondered? Oh, poor Frederick, she said to herself in her head, I'm sorry, so sorry.

She was far too intelligent really to suppose that what had happened to Frederick was her fault, but she nevertheless always had a sneaking feeling that in a way, somewhere along the line, she was the tiniest bit responsible. If she had behaved differently could she not somehow have altered things? But then she would remember again the shame of the drunken, incoherent sermons, the humiliation of forgotten parish meetings, congregations kept waiting, flirtations with the lady of the manor – blue eyes flashing – and then she would want to blot it all out, to wish that it had never happened, to wish that he, Frederick, had never existed. But then there were the children. And then again she would see those two men standing side by side – the good one and the bad one.

'Gatey,' she said, 'I'm exhausted. Let's go to bed. We can talk again tomorrow.' She really wanted to ask Gatey about her life, her boyfriend, her future. Not to talk so much about herself.

It rained all that night and in the morning water was pouring through the ceiling into Percy Hardcastle's bedroom. He appeared in a rage and sent Sylvia to put a bucket in the room to catch the drips. Needless to say, Gatey wondered why on earth he couldn't carry a bucket upstairs for himself? He told Sylvia that a man would be coming later to look at the roof, would she stay in for him?

Gatey was livid. Why should they have to stay in for that? Sylvia thought it was perfectly reasonable, and anyway they couldn't possibly want to go anywhere on such a horrible day.

It was a Saturday so Sylvia had to cook lunch as well as supper for Hardcastle. He had said earlier in the week that he was expecting Jocelyn for the weekend, but she did not appear to have turned up.

'I shall be preaching in the village church tomorrow,' he said to Sylvia, as she laid the usual solitary place for him at the kitchen table.

Sylvia thought that she must have misheard him.

'Preach? Did you say preach?' she asked him.

'Preach indeed. Preach,' he replied. 'I have the honour of being a lay preacher and as such am often called upon in the neighbourhood. I hope that you will come to hear my few humble words of wisdom. Eleven o'clock matins. Book of Common Prayer.'

Since separating from Frederick, Sylvia had rather given up going to church. She wasn't exactly sure what she thought about the existence of God – not that she thought about Him very often – but she had definitely given up believing in any form of organised religion. In any case, anything to do with church made her feel rather uncomfortable and evoked too many awkward memories. She certainly had no intention of going to listen to Percy Hardcastle preaching. The very idea appalled her. She was quite amazed to learn that he was a lay preacher. On second thoughts, perhaps she wasn't so amazed. She had seen some rum ones in her time, men who loved the sound of their own voices.

'I must have told you before that I am a lay preacher,' Hardcastle remarked. 'I have to say in all humility that I am rather proud of the fact. God indeed moves in a mysterious way for Him to have chosen me as His mouthpiece.' He looked at the place Sylvia had laid for his lunch and said suddenly and with feeling, 'No Jocelyn.' Then he turned and walked out of the kitchen. A moment later he came back with a glass of what looked like whisky in his hand. 'It's rather chilly this morning,' he said, 'I think I need a little something to warm me up.' Then he asked Sylvia, 'How can I make her come? How did you get your daughter to come?'

Sylvia immediately felt terribly sorry for him and almost as if she ought to apologise for Gatey being there at all.

'She doesn't come very often,' she said gently. But she knew of no comforting words to add.

'So what's this Jocelyn like?' Gatey asked her mother over lunch.

'Beautiful, apparently,' said Sylvia.

'Sounds like a bitch to me,' said Gatey. 'Her father's pretty horrid, but it is her father. You'd think she could come and see him sometimes when he's all alone and a widower.'

Sylvia thought of Evidence and wanted to weep. She wondered if Gatey preached to him.

It cleared up in the afternoon and Sylvia took Prophecy for a walk, leaving Gatey watching an old Bette Davis film on television. She promised to look out for the man about the roof, but he didn't turn up until Sylvia came back. She found him in the yard, a small, pale, wiry man with a lined face, looking rather worried. He'd unblocked all the gutters and the gulleys in the roof quite recently and wondered where the trouble was coming from. Perhaps a tile had blown off in the night?

Wilf Wapshott knew the house well, he'd been looking after it for Mr Hardcastle for at least twenty years now. The roof was always giving trouble, what with loose tiles and that, but the gulleys and the gutters were a pesky nuisance, you'd no sooner cleared the leaves out of them than they were blocked up again.

'Well,' he said, 'we'll have to see what we can do. They say there's more rain on the way.'

Sylvia took him indoors and upstairs to Percy Hardcastle's bedroom to see where the water had been coming in. He looked at the ceiling, nodded and asked for a bucket and then, bucket in hand, he disappeared onto the landing and up into the loft. In no time he was

43

on the roof, and before very long Sylvia saw him reappear with his bucket full of leaves.

'I think that ought to do the trick,' he said.

Sylvia looked at him and vaguely wondered how old he was. He certainly moved with the agility of a monkey but, she thought, he must be pushing sixty. She looked at her watch.

'I was just about to put the kettle on,' she said. 'Would you like a cup of tea?'

Gatey and Sylvia and Wilf sat round Sylvia's kitchen table drinking thick tea from mugs. Gatey was determined to find out more about the Hardcastles. Sylvia thought she pried a little and was slightly embarrassed by the conversation, but curious nevertheless.

'So what was Mrs Hardcastle like?' Gatey wanted to know. She was sitting forward, with her mug in both hands, her chin thrust out and her eyes wide open – intent.

'Mrs Hardcastle was a lovely lady,' said Wilf. 'A lovely lady. Always spoke nicely to everyone – whoever they were. Always stopped for a word if you met her in the village.'

'And do you think,' Gatey asked, leaning even further forward, 'that he was a wife beater?'

'Gatey, don't be so silly!' Sylvia spoke sharply.

'Well, he might have been,' said Gatey. 'They do exist you know, Mum – in all classes.'

'Now that is something we never shall know,' said Wilf. 'If he was, I reckon he'll take the secret to his grave now.'

'So you think he was!' Gatey's eyes were wider open than ever and her face was alight with excitement.

Wilf just laughed and stirred the sugar in his tea.

'But what did she die of?' Gatey wanted to know.

'Cancer,' said Wilf. 'She died the same summer as the wife.'

Gatey barely paused in her enquiries to allow her mother to make suitably sympathetic noises, but for a moment Wilf's attention was distracted from Gatey.

'It was terrible,' he said. 'I didn't know how I'd go on, but you do in the end.'

'So you do think he was a wife beater?' Gatey came back to her point.

'Now I never said that,' Wilf grinned.

'Well, what about this Jocelyn?' Gatey wanted to know next.

'Jocelyn? We don't see much of her these days,' said Wilf, but he would say no more.

When Wilf had gone Sylvia was quite cross with Gatey. It really would not do for Sylvia, in her position, to be heard gossiping about her employer in the village.

Gatey just laughed. Wilf was a nice man and he obviously didn't mind. In fact, he thought it was funny.

'That's not the point,' said Sylvia.

'But,' said Gatey earnestly, 'don't you think Mr Hardcastle really must have been a wife beater?'

Sylvia thought Gatey was being ridiculous. You couldn't just accuse everyone you disliked of the most appalling crimes.

Gatey said, 'You're an innocent, Mum,' and sighed.

The next day Gatey left after lunch and as her train drew out of Battle station Sylvia wiped a tear from her eye. She would miss her – life without her was very dull and of course she wondered when she would see her again. She wondered if in fact she would see Gatey or Evidence or Jocelyn next. Gatey probably wouldn't be back in a hurry as Sylvia, who had bought her her railway ticket, had tried to make her promise not to hitch-hike any more. But Gatey insisted that it was the only form of travel she could afford.

'The trouble is,' Sylvia said heavily to Prophecy that night, 'our next visitor is going to be my mother and that will wear us both out, won't it?'

Prophecy just wagged her tail, but Sylvia felt depressed and guilty and angry as she plodded wearily upstairs to bed.

IV

When Lady Field heard that Gatey had been to stay with Sylvia she was perfectly furious.

Over the years Sylvia had learned to foretell with infallible accuracy what her mother's reaction would be to any given circumstance, and to know precisely what would ignite the inevitable explosion of manipulative self-pity and jealousy. Fear of the consequences often prevented her from telephoning Lady Field, or indeed of telling her, when she did telephone, the smallest, most unimportant detail of her life. Sometimes she felt a sickening dread hanging over her as the days passed and the moment which she could no longer put off drew nearer. But sometimes she herself felt so lonely that she longed to hear the sound of a familiar voice, even her mother's, and to feel that she belonged somewhere.

Sylvia didn't telephone her mother until the following Thursday.

'I must admit,' said Lady Field sharply as soon as she heard Sylvia's voice, 'I had begun to forget that I had a daughter. What have you been doing that was so important that you couldn't even ring your mother?'

'Oh Mummy, I'm so sorry.' Sylvia began her usual stream of abject apologies. 'I really am dreadfully sorry, but you see Gatey came down to stay . . .' As she mentioned Gatey she realised it was a mistake.

'How lovely for you,' Lady Field's voice rang with icy insincerity, 'to have been surrounded by your family. I haven't seen or spoken to a soul for days,' her voice faded away into a weak, trembly mode.

'Well she was only here for a night,' Sylvia lied, and backtracked pathetically.

'She never comes to see her grandmother, but of course the young are so selfish these days. Then you never come to see me either. In fact, I can hardly remember what you look like.'

Sylvia wanted to scream – why did she have to put up with this nonsense year in and year out? And why did it always make her feel so guilty? Couldn't her mother see that she had only just settled into a new job, that her life had been in a state of flux, that it wasn't easy for her to go running up and down the country? More than that, would she ever understand that her very behaviour made one wish never to see her? If anyone else had ever behaved towards Sylvia half as vilely as her mother had done, she would long ago have ceased to have anything to do with them.

Heaving with guilt at the bitter resentment which she felt towards her mother, Sylvia tried again.

'Mummy,' she said, 'I'm so sorry, I really am; it's awful for you to feel so lonely – really beastly, I know, but it won't be long now until you come to stay.'

'I don't think I shall be coming,' said Lady Field.

'Oh, why not? Do come . . . it will be lovely for me.' Another lie.

'It's too difficult, I can't travel any more and there's

no one to feed the cat. I'll just stay here . . . alone. No one wants an old woman.'

'Well I'll ring you up again in a few days' time to see how you are feeling about it,' Sylvia said weakly. There was nothing else she could do.

When Lady Field had finished talking to Sylvia she rang her neighbour – the one with a full-time job, an unemployed husband, a senile mother-in-law, a retarded teenager and who drove so dangerously – and ordered her to take her to the station on the day appointed for her trip to Sussex. Then she rang her other neighbour and instructed her to feed the cat while she was away. She wondered whether to ring Milly next or not. She wanted Milly to do something for her, but she had no idea what. Besides, there was something else that she might want to tell Milly, but she wasn't sure whether the time was ripe for that yet. What a nuisance that Gatey didn't have a telephone. She was furious with Gatey. Perhaps she would write to her, but then, she thought bitterly, the child is probably illiterate. The trouble with Gatey was that her mother had always spoilt her and given her everything she wanted so that it never occurred to her to think of anyone else but herself. She had taken after her father too, which was a great pity. Lady Field had never had any time for Frederick. Indeed, she had been quite relieved when the marriage broke up. Sylvia and Frederick had certainly never been suited to each other – Lady Field had told them so from the very start – but they would know best. For one thing Frederick was far too clever for Sylvia; it must have been very difficult for him to run a parish and do all the things that a clergyman has to do, with an unintelligent wife dragging him down all the time.

Now Lady Field would have loved to have married

an intelligent man like Frederick, instead of someone as stupid as Kenneth. She had very little time for Frederick, very little time indeed, but she did feel for him in one respect. She knew what it was like to be tied to someone stupider than yourself. That could have been one of the reasons why Frederick had taken to the bottle, although to be perfectly fair to the man, Lady Field had always been of the opinion that Sylvia exaggerated grossly about that. Probably in order to excuse her own behaviour in some peculiar way. God only knew what had been happening to Frederick since the divorce. Anyway, in her mother's opinion Sylvia had never been capable of great self-knowledge – not at all like Lady Field. One thing about Lady Field was that she did know her own limitations. So very few people did.

She decided that she probably would write to Gatey as it really was time the child learned a few home truths. Perhaps it would help her to face up to life, to learn to think of others, and she might even stop and think and realise what a wise woman her grandmother was. Lady Field imagined Gatey, having received the letter, hurrying down to Manchester to stay with her grandmother where she would be full of remorse for her past errors and eager to learn at the knees of the oracle. She might even move in with her grandmother and get a little job. That would teach Sylvia. It would really be quite convenient having Gatey to live with her so long as she understood that she would not be allowed to smoke, or to use the bathroom. She could do some housework and the shopping. Lady Field felt quite cheerful at the prospect of it all.

Sylvia was not feeling nearly so cheerful for her part. She hardly dared hope that her mother might really cancel her visit, because the pattern was already so familiar. In the end she would, as she had always done before, patiently welcome her mother and silently submit to whatever insults the old lady chose to hurl in her direction for the duration of her stay. She wondered again why it was that she had never really stood up to her mother and why, at the age of fifty-something, she still allowed herself to be terrorised and bullied by her. Again, she was reminded of Frederick, years ago in the early days of their marriage, saying to her, 'For God's sake stand up to your mother! Tell her to fuck off . . .'

In those days Sylvia had been shocked by such bad language, especially coming as it did from a priest. She was also shocked at the idea of being anything but a dutiful, loving, grateful daughter. She could no more have rebuked her own mother than she could have slit her own throat. Now she felt more attracted to both lines of action. How she wished she had taken Frederick's advice years ago! Now it was too late, but in those days she had quite simply swallowed her mother's line about herself, excusing her behaviour on the grounds that Lady Field had had such a hard time with Sylvia's father and that now she was alone and lonely with only her daughter to care for her. It never entered her head to question whether or not her mother really cared for her.

Now she could no longer understand how it was that she had put up with so much then. It occurred to her that she had never ever questioned her mother's right to hurt or dominate her. And still she accepted it. Visions from the past rose before her eyes in unending succession . . .

She remembered bringing Frederick home for the first time when she was dreadfully in love with him. Frederick was tall and then he was good-looking, almost too thin, with a puckered, rather anxious look on his face. It was this puckered, anxious look that she had initially found particularly attractive in him. He seemed to be a mixture of pride and diffidence which was rather attractive too, and he was peculiarly apologetic about being in the Church as if he didn't know quite how or why he had got there and as if it might all be a most awful mistake anyway. Sylvia thought he was wonderful. She also thought that he was quite incredibly clever, the way he was always reading things like Voltaire and Rilke in the original. In retrospect she saw a tortured young man, full of self-doubt, who probably had no idea what he was up to. Then she had seen a hero. Poor old Frederick, she thought, and vaguely wondered what he was up to now.

When Frederick came to supper on that first occasion, Lady Field had been all over him, asking him briefly about himself and telling him at length about herself and about what a hard time she had had with Sir Kenneth. She envied him his talent for languages – Sylvia had told her that he spoke French and German fluently – and told him that she herself would have very much liked to learn foreign languages as she felt she had an ear for them. Sylvia, on the other hand, had no ear – no gift for languages at all and had always been bottom of the class in French – 'weren't you, darling?'

Sylvia could hear that, 'Weren't you, darling?' all these years later as clearly as if it had only just dropped from her mother's lips. Why, she wondered, did it still hurt? Why couldn't she just forgive and forget, or quite simply, even at this late stage, tell her mother, in Frederick's words, to fuck off?

When Frederick had left after that first evening, Lady Field had really put the knife in. She didn't feel that Sylvia ought to expect too much from that young man because, in Lady Field's opinion, he was what they used to call 'not the marrying kind', and besides he was clearly unstable. In any case, even if he were the marrying kind, Sylvia was not likely to be his type – she was certainly not clever enough, for one thing, and not glamorous enough, for another. Too colourless and dumpy. To tell the truth, Lady Field had always been a little disappointed at not having a clever child, and as for the other – well it never did anyone any good to be too glamorous.

Sylvia wanted to stop thinking about her mother and about the past. None of it helped. It only increased her own loneliness and sense of inadequacy and cast her into a depression. 'Poor Mummy,' she tried to think, 'she obviously doesn't realise she's doing it – and she has had an awfully difficult life.'

She turned on the television. She didn't care what was on, but somehow she must block out her own interminably repetitive thoughts. She spent too much time on her own. Perhaps that was what had happened to her mother.

'Come on Prophecy,' she said, 'let's think of something else for a change.' She wanted to think of something positive, but whichever way she looked she seemed to come up against a blank wall. The television did nothing to improve matters because she was finding it impossible to concentrate or to take in what was being said. When she stopped thinking about her mother she began thinking about Evidence or Gatey. When she thought about Evidence she felt sad and when she thought about Gatey she felt worried. If she thought about her job and congratulated herself on having found it and on having somewhere at least halfway decent to live, then she began to think about Percy Hardcastle and what a really not very nice man he was and to

53

worry about how closely involved she would have to become with him. Then she thought about her own sense of isolation again and wondered whether she preferred to spend more time with someone she didn't really like or more time alone. Then she wondered how she might set about meeting people in the village or the neighbourhood and then she knew that she hadn't the strength to make the effort and she began to feel close to despair. But there must be so many other people all over the country in a situation similar to hers. Her poor old mother for one.

Sylvia patted the sofa beside her and invited Prophecy to jump up on it. Then she put both her arms round the dog's neck, buried her face in its massive head and drew comfort from the presence of so warm and faithful a creature.

'So many caterpillars,' she said. 'We are just all so many caterpillars crawling over the surface of the earth for no apparent reason.'

Sometimes when Sylvia was thinking about caterpillars crawling on the surface of the earth, she found it quite impossible to comprehend why they all minded everything so much if they were only caterpillars, and then she herself began to think that nothing mattered. Nothing at all. Nor love, nor loyalty, nor truth, nor honour – only Prophecy. She tightened her hold round the dog's neck.

The next morning Sylvia dragged herself out of bed rather wondering how she would ever get through the day. The sky was heavy and grey and there was very little light. If only the sun would sometimes shine, she thought. She made herself a cup of tea and then went next door to cook Percy Hardcastle his regular breakfast of fried eggs and bacon. As often as not he smeared the eggs round the plate and hid the bacon under his knife and fork, having eaten no more than a mouthful. Too much to drink the night before, Sylvia supposed.

Hardcastle was already in the kitchen making himself a cup of coffee with shaking hands. A sash-cord was broken on one of the sitting-room windows, he told her.

'Give little Wilf Wapshott a ring, will you,' he said, 'and get him to come and see to it as soon as possible.'

Sylvia winced at the patronising manner.

Later in the morning a ray of sunshine broke through the heavy cloud and lifted Sylvia's spirits very slightly, but not enough to prevent her from still dreading the arrival of Wilf. He was a perfectly nice man, but she really did not feel up to any form of polite chatter with anyone and she supposed that she would have to offer him a cup of tea. She wanted to be able to make an effort, but she genuinely felt that the energy required just to perform her minimal daily tasks was colossal. She wondered if she was ill.

Wilf arrived in the early part of the afternoon and took some time fixing the window. By the time he had finished, Sylvia was feeling distinctly more alive and was even quite looking forward to offering him a cup of tea. She wondered if it wasn't just the effect of there being another person in the house doing something which made her feel better.

Wilf was quite ready for his cup of tea which he drank slowly before gladly accepting a second one. By the time he finally left for home Sylvia was horrified to realise that they had been chatting round her kitchen table for nearly two hours. She wondered what they had talked about – certainly the time had flown. Wilf had told her about his wife and about how difficult he had found it to come to terms with her death, but he had managed to come to terms with it in the end and now he was quite happy – contented at least – in his cottage in the village. Got a bit lonely at times, but he could cope with that now. They'd had no children which hadn't really bothered him until the wife died. He'd felt the draught then. These days he put all his energies into his work, did a bit of gardening, occasionally put something on a horse. He winked.

'My son was called after a horse that won the 3.30 at Lincoln on the day he was born,' Sylvia couldn't help admitting.

Wilf was delighted by the information.

'His father won a lot of money on it – it was an outsider,' she added, but something somehow restrained her from revealing that she had been married to a clergyman. That piece of information, she had learned long ago, often had a very peculiar effect on people. It usually made them clam up and presume that you had no sense of humour. She told Wilf that she was divorced, but no more than that. Later they spoke about Gatey, and Sylvia was surprised to find herself confiding her worries about her daughter to this comparative stranger.

As far as Wilf knew everyone these days had trouble with their children. 'Look at next door,' he said, nodding towards the dividing wall.

'She hasn't been down since I've been here,' Sylvia said.

'Never comes down if she can help it as far as I can see,' said Wilf.

Sylvia wondered why.

'It's a mystery to me,' said Wilf. 'She's a beautiful girl and he's given her everything. Too much, if you ask me, he's probably spoilt her. Or perhaps she's with an unsuitable bloke. Who knows?'

'Well I can't wait to see this great beauty,' said Sylvia.

'Mind you,' Wilf went on, 'I don't expect he's all that easy.' He nodded his head towards the dividing wall again. 'The lady who was here before you, she didn't stay long, and as for the one before that, she hardly stopped to unpack her bags. There's been dozens of them.'

Sylvia was rather embarrassed. She really must not discuss Mr Hardcastle, particularly since she herself could think of nothing very nice to say about him.

'Nobody likes him much in the village,' said Wilf. 'Gives himself airs, thinks he's better than the rest of us, that's his trouble. Preaches in the church as if he was God Almighty they say. Still, I shouldn't say any more – at least he pays his bills on time.'

When Wilf had left, Sylvia realised that she was missing his friendly presence. Funny what a little company could do for you. Perhaps Wilf was lonely too. She glanced at the window – it was nearly dark outside – and she imagined Wilf going back alone to his cottage. She didn't in fact know which his cottage was. She must ask someone sometime.

That evening Percy Hardcastle asked Sylvia to stay and eat supper with him. She didn't want to do so but could think of no excuse which would be remotely polite. It was the first time that he had insisted on her staying, but she had felt it coming for a little while and knowing that he, like herself, must be lonely she thought it unkind to refuse, but sincerely hoped that it would not become a regular obligation. Wherever she looked she saw acres of loneliness.

As the evening drew on Hardcastle grew more and more drunken and more and more maudlin. His eyes glazed over and he drooled on endlessly and incoherently about Jocelyn.

Sylvia could hardly bear it. She had had quite enough drunken, bleary-eyed talk from Frederick, but at least Frederick had originally been a sympathetic and interesting man. She rather doubted that the same could be said of Percy Hardcastle. Suddenly she smiled to herself at the memory of Frederick's drunken drooling. She had never thought it remotely funny before, but his confused musing about Hegel and Nietzsche were a far cry from this man's obsessive love for his daughter, although in the end it all added up to the same thing.

Sylvia was wondering how long it would be before she could decently make her getaway when she noticed tears rolling down Hardcastle's cheeks. He pulled a handkerchief out of his pocket and blew his nose loudly, then staggered to his feet and lurched out of the room to replenish his glass. Sylvia was quite worried that he might fall down or collapse before getting back to the table. She knew there was no point in her trying to say anything about his not needing another drink. She had gone through all that – the watered-down bottles of whisky, the threats, the pleas, the lectures – and she knew from bitter experience that there was absolutely nothing anyone could do to stop another person from drinking. Perhaps Jocelyn had learned that too at an early age and perhaps that was what kept her away.

Hardcastle came back, slopping whisky from a brimming glass and slumped into his chair. He was still crying.

Sylvia was moved to put out her hand and touch him.

'Are you all right?' she asked gently, although she could see perfectly well that he was very far from all right.

Perhaps it was her movement towards him which made him break. Perhaps no one had been remotely kind or outgoing towards him for a very long time indeed. Whatever it was, his shoulders suddenly began to heave and a strangled sob was shaken from his chest. He put his elbows on the table and buried his head in his hands, his white hair fell forward, his whole body shuddered and from somewhere in the midst of the heaving mass a faint voice almost whispered, 'I'm a failure.'

She had heard that before too and despite her pity she just wanted to run away, to go next door and to curl up on the floor or the sofa with Prophecy. She began to understand why people often said inanely that they preferred animals to people.

She stood up and did – despite herself – remove the untouched glass of whisky, and as she did so she heard herself say, like a schoolmistress, 'I think you've had enough of that. I'll make you some coffee.'

Gradually Hardcastle stopped sobbing, he blew his nose again and made some sort of half-hearted effort to pull himself together.

'It's her,' he said as Sylvia put a cup of strong coffee beside him. 'It's all her fault. Have you ever loved anyone, Sylvia? I love her more than I love life and she hates me – otherwise she'd come and see me – you know she would, don't you?'

'I've no idea,' said Sylvia helplessly.

'I've killed her – killed her love,' he said, 'and you should see her – the most perfect figure – perfect – perfect,' he drooled on.

There was nothing that Sylvia could do. She certainly couldn't see herself getting that mountain of a man upstairs to bed, so she would have to leave him sitting where he was and just hope that he wouldn't be there in the morning when she came through to make his breakfast. She knew that in the morning he would either have forgotten this evening's scene, or he would pretend to have done so. He would be his usual pompous, rather overbearing self. She drew consolation from the fact that a niggling sense of discomfort might prevent him from asking her to have supper with him again for a very long time. And she was certainly not altogether surprised to have found out that she had come at the end of a long line of housekeepers, and wondered how long she would be able to stick it.

'I must go,' she said, 'I wouldn't have any more to drink, if I were you.' She wondered why she bothered to waste her breath.

Back in her own side of the house Sylvia began to brood on what Hardcastle had said. This obsession with Jocelyn was quite overwhelming, he couldn't keep off the subject, drunk or sober. But what was he getting at when he said that he had killed her love? And why in the long run did she never come near him, or, as far as Sylvia could tell, even ring him?

The most peculiar thing of all about the whole evening as far as Sylvia was concerned was that it made her think of Frederick in a more affectionate way than she had done for a very long time. A very long time indeed. She even found herself missing him, and wishing that she could talk to him about Hardcastle. One day perhaps he would turn up again. Yes, she thought, she would definitely like to see him – as long as he wasn't too drunk.

As she had expected, Hardcastle was his usual bluff and pompous self in the morning. It was a Saturday so he wouldn't be going to work, but he announced that he would be out for the day and wouldn't be wanting any lunch. He made no attempt whatsoever to eat his eggs and bacon.

Another long and empty day stretched ahead of

Sylvia so that she even wondered if her mother's proposed visit wouldn't be an improvement on these eternal hours of solitude – and it was raining again as usual.

At eleven o'clock Wilf turned up, saying that he had left a chisel behind when he fixed the window. Sylvia was pleased to see him as his visit, however short, would break into the monotony of the day. She found him his chisel and made him a cup of tea. They sat and talked for another hour before he had to be on his way and Sylvia was tempted to tell him about the events of the previous evening, but she held back, still feeling that she owed her loyalty to Hardcastle. Wilf suddenly seemed to represent an island of sanity in an otherwise mad world, and he had an easy humour and detached manner, both of which she found attractive.

'Any time you're passing,' she said as he left, 'you can always look in for a cup of tea.' She felt comfortable with Wilf.

V

Gatey was still asleep when the postman arrived. In fact she didn't wake up until very late that morning. She hadn't gone to bed until four o'clock anyway and had probably smoked too many joints. When she did wake she had very little desire to get up, instead she stretched out an arm and turned on the radio. Her boyfriend was not in the bed and it struck her that the rest of the house felt pretty empty. When she did eventually get out of bed she found that she was in fact alone in the house. She wondered vaguely where all the others had gone. Not very many of them went to work.

It was lucky really that she found the letter at all. It lay inside the door with a lot of the usual junk mail, that habitually lay there until the pile became too high for the front door to be opened and had been trodden on by muddy boots going in and out. It felt pretty fat and she could not imagine what her grandmother, whose writing she recognised, could possibly have to say to her, but she felt sure that it would be quite annoying. She decided not to open it until she had had some coffee. Even then she wondered if she would be bothered to read it. Not if it was going to be one long complaint.

Perhaps it was because she didn't get many letters that Gatey eventually decided to savour this one, even if it was going to be annoying. It took her some time to make some coffee mainly because she couldn't find a mug as they were all dirty and piled in the sink. Well, there were a couple on the floor with cigarettes stubbed out in them. Rather than wash one up she decided to drink her coffee out of the only container she could find which was an empty milk bottle. It turned out to be a somewhat inconvenient vessel as when she tipped it up to her mouth the hot coffee trickled down her cheeks and down her neck. She couldn't really be bothered with the coffee any more so she abandoned the milk bottle and rolled a cigarette and took it back to bed with her letter.

Gatey was completely amazed and somewhat annoyed by what she read and, for a moment, non-plussed as to what to do about it. But it was not long before she decided that the only thing to do was to go to Manchester as quickly as possible. She must see Evidence at once.

She got out of bed and dressed, then shoved a few things she would need into a plastic bag and was ready to go. As she left the house she bumped into one of her friends coming back with a friend of his who might have been able to connect the electricity for them, bypassing the electricity board. That would mean hot water from the immersion heater for a bath.

'Good,' said Gatey. 'I'm going to Manchester.'

'When'll you be back?' her friend asked.

'Dunno,' said Gatey and she was gone.

She was lucky to hitch a lift quite quickly from a lorry driver at a service station on the North Circular. She might have had to wait for hours, although it wasn't usually too bad. The driver didn't seem to be a particularly communicative sort so Gatey decided to re-read her grandmother's letter.

Darling Gatey,
I have been sick with worry about you for some time now, and after considerable thought have at last decided that the time has come for me to write. You should, I feel, realise that your way of life gives cause for very great concern to both your mother and me and it is high time that you learned to face up to the realities of this world and to consider others before yourself. Unfortunately you are the child of weak parents who have been unable to give you a properly stable background such as the one which I (at great personal expense) was able to give to your mother. Furthermore, I think it my duty to point out to you that you have, through no fault of your own, inherited some of the worst aspects of your father's character. This is made palpably obvious from your casual attitude to life and your inability to think of anyone but your little self.

As your grandmother, and an older and wiser person, I feel that I have every right to point all this out to you and I am sure that you will have at least enough sense to pay careful attention to what I say, as I cannot believe that you sincerely wish to continue blindly hurting your family in the way you do.

It is, I must add, a great shame that along with your father's weaknesses you have also inherited the high-handed thoughtlessness and egoism of your mother and her lack of imagination. Had you any imagination, I suppose that you might sometimes allow it to dwell on my loneliness. I feel that I have had very little thanks for a life devoted to the welfare of my family. Have you ever considered what a dreadful blow it was to me when your mother married your father?

> With love from
> Yr affectionate Granny

P.S. I am not sure whether I ought to tell you that I
have some news of your father who is not well at all.

'Silly bitch!' Gatey declared.

The lorry driver looked a little surprised and, in his
curiosity, became rather more communicative himself.
His grandmother was a wicked old lady too. She'd
lived with his mum and dad all their married life and
never given them a moment's peace; he sometimes
wondered why one of them hadn't ever murdered her.
She'd done enough to deserve it.

Once they had begun to compare grandmothers the
rest of the journey passed quite quickly and they were
soon in Manchester.

Gatey was not at all sure what Evidence would
have to say when he saw Lady Field's letter and neither
was she in the least bit decided about whether or not
they would tell their mother about it. It would be
sure to upset her and make her very angry indeed, but
more particularly, what would she think or feel about
what it said about their father? What indeed did Gatey
herself feel about that? First and foremost she was
absolutely furious that any news of her father should
reach her through her grandmother. She wondered if
Evidence knew what it was all about and she wondered
too how on earth Lady Field could have any information whatsoever concerning her father or his whereabouts.

It was at least three years since Gatey had seen
Frederick. At the time he had been in London and was
applying for a job as a traffic warden. She never knew
whether or not he got the job and, although in part of
her being she felt that she loved him, she in fact thought
about him very little. She loved him for the good times,
mostly remembered from early childhood when her

65

father would do sudden, quirky things like taking her racing on a day when she was supposed to be at school, or reading aloud to her from a strange, unsuitable book, his eyes flashing, his mellow voice filled with emotion. Or, sometimes, in a burst of enthusiasm he would take them all to the zoo, or fishing, or kite flying. Whatever it was, it always depended on a whim and was always invested with tremendous *joie de vivre* until the terrible moment when the pandas wouldn't wake up, or the fish wouldn't be caught, or the wind dropped and then the mood would change. A dejected and despondent family would pile back into the little car and drive silently home.

As time went on the enthusiasm and the *joie de vivre* were gradually replaced by irritability and bad temper, depression, rage, despair. Times were bad and Gatey used to do her level best to avoid being at home, or if she was there she would hide away for as long as possible in her bedroom. Sometimes she overhead terrible rows between her parents and quite often she knew that her father had hit her mother. Then she hated and despised them both for making her so unhappy, and him for being drunk, and her for putting up with his violence.

When her parents eventually separated she was heartily relieved. Then as the years went by and she looked back on what had been, she began to feel very sorry for her father. It was easier now that he was no longer around to inflict pain and she would think again of the fishing or the kite flying or the strange, unsuitable books and think of what might have been and of how, if it weren't for the drink, he could have been a bishop or something by now. Not that she was particularly impressed by the idea of a bishop, but she liked to think that her father could have reached the top of his chosen profession. Sometimes she wondered why he of all people had picked that particular profession, but it always made her angry when her mother said that she wasn't absolutely sure that he had ever been entirely convinced by the divinity of Christ. It was not that Frederick was a hypocrite, Sylvia assured her, but that a tireless intellectual search for the truth had left him somewhat bemused.

Gatey wasn't at all sure whether she would find anyone in or not when she turned up so unexpectedly at Evidence's house. If no one was there she would just go away and moon around the shops in Manchester until the evening, by which time she could expect to find Milly at home. She wasn't in the least bit worried as she had done this sort of thing before. But this time she turned out to be lucky. She had just satisfied herself that no one was at home and was walking away slowly down the street, miles away in her mind, when she suddenly heard her name called. She looked up and there coming towards her at the end of the street was Milly with a pile of shopping.

'Lovely to see you Gatey!' Milly exclaimed as she drew nearer. 'What are you doing? Lucky you caught me – I'd just gone out to do some shopping. Come on in.' Gatey followed Milly inside and was delighted to discover that her sister-in-law had some days off work. Milly was really pleased to see Gatey.

'I've had this filthy letter from Granny,' Gatey said as she and Milly sat at the kitchen table with mugs of coffee. 'She really is a cow, you know.'

'To tell you the truth,' Milly said, 'she doesn't bother me because she's not my grandmother, but I think she's getting worse. The other day she managed to get me to go all the way over there just to buy her a tin of cat food. I can't think why I went, but you can't say no, somehow. Evidence was furious – and he won't go anywhere near her. I think it's a bit mean of him really. I suppose that's why I go instead – I feel sorry for her.'

'I don't feel at all sorry for her,' Gatey was emphatic.

'She's old and lonely,' said Milly.

'Serve her right,' said Gatey, fishing in her plastic bag for Lady Field's letter. 'Just wait till you've seen this. It's vile. Absolutely vile.' She retrieved the letter from among a pair of green pants, a packet of rizlas and some spot cream, all of which she put on the table in turn. 'And,' she said, handing the letter to Milly, 'has she said anything to you or Evidence about my father?'

'No,' said Milly, taking the letter. 'Certainly not to me, and I doubt she's spoken to Evidence. I think he'd have said something if she had.'

'Do you know where he is?'

'Evidence? He's at work,' said Milly.

'No, not Evidence,' said Gatey, 'my father.'

'No,' said Milly, 'I don't. We've never heard from him, and Evidence never mentions him. You know what he's like, he doesn't want to know anything about his family, except for you of course; I even think he's rather bad about your mother. He doesn't ring her very often.'

'I know,' said Gatey, 'he's a bit of a pig sometimes. But read Granny's letter.' She rolled herself a cigarette.

'You'd better be careful with those when Evidence gets back,' Milly nodded towards Gatey's cigarette, 'Evidence won't allow anyone to smoke in the house any more.'

'Oh God,' Gatey moaned and dragged at her cigarette. 'I don't think I'll pay any attention to that.'

Milly laughed. 'I've got a couple of nursing friends who come here and chain smoke. It makes him livid. He goes on and on about it, but you'd be surprised how

68

many nurses do smoke.' Milly unfolded the letter and began to read.

Gatey sat fuming at the prospect of her brother making her go out into the garden to smoke. Evidence could be a pill at times.

Milly was amazed by what she read. How could anyone write such a horrible letter to their grandchild? She thought of her own grandmother who had died a year ago. She was a proper grandmother, who knitted jerseys for you and baked cakes and biscuits and took you to the zoo and who thought that all her grand-children were perfect. Lady Field would never cease to surprise Milly.

'But how can she possibly know anything about your father?' she asked Gatey when she had finished reading. 'Why should she know where he is?'

'God knows,' said Gatey. 'I want to know what Evidence is going to say, but I'm not at all sure what I'm going to do. I suppose I'll have to go and see Granny and ask her what it's all about. But I want Evidence to come with me.'

'I hope he will,' said Milly, but she knew it would be hard to persuade him.

'The thing is,' said Gatey, 'I really don't want to play into her hands. I mean, you know how darned manip-ulative she is – and that letter is a trap of some sort. I absolutely refuse to fall into Granny's traps.'

'I think,' said Milly thoughtfully, 'that the whole letter was written for the sake of the postscript. I mean, she really thought that by saying something about your father – and not telling you what – she'd have got your attention.' Milly threw the letter down on the table and looked long and hard at Gatey. 'But I simply don't know what you should do,' she said.

'Well if Dad's really ill, someone ought to go to him,

whatever he's done,' said Gatey. 'You see, if he did want to get in touch with one of us, he'd find it impossible. He's no idea where we live. How does she know anything about him?' Gatey paused for a moment and then added, 'Silly bitch.'

'Don't do anything until you've talked to Evidence,' Milly said.

'I hope he'll do something for once,' said Gatey. 'I don't want to go and see Granny on my own, I might kill her. And do you know,' she went on, 'that the father of the lorry driver who gave me a lift down wanted to kill his mother-in-law. The lorry driver was amazed that he didn't. Actually I'm surprised more people don't get murdered. I mean, half of them don't deserve to live.'

'Steady on,' said Milly.

By the time Evidence came back from work Gatey had decided that whatever happened she must force him to go with her to see their grandmother, unless Lady Field was prepared to talk over the telephone, which Gatey doubted. The bait was too good. If Gatey could persuade Evidence to go with her she felt he might add some gravitas to the situation. He was so much better at keeping his cool than she was. She could imagine herself flying off the handle at the first barbed remark, however much she intended to remain calm. Besides, Evidence hardly ever saw Lady Field who was anyway a little in awe of him and who would prefer to remain in his good books if she could. This meant that she would undoubtedly have to tread a little more carefully if Evidence was there, and if Lady Field felt a little uncomfortable she would be all the easier to deal with.

When Evidence came home Milly was preparing tea in the kitchen and Gatey was sitting at the table having another cigarette. He came into the kitchen and wrinkled up his nose, sniffing in disapproval.

'Gatey!' he exclaimed, 'what are you doing here? You're welcome of course, so long as you put that awful cigarette out. You should have told her that this is a smoke-free zone,' he added, turning to Milly and giving her a kiss on the cheek.

'Oh come on Evidence, don't be so pompous,' said Gatey and she took a last aggressive puff at her almost-finished cigarette before unwillingly grinding it out in her matchbox.

'Do you realise that four million working hours are wasted every year in this country as a result of tobacco related diseases?' said Evidence sternly. 'And, furthermore, do you realise that smoking damages the skin, the hair, the toenails, that it causes sterility, deafness, irritation of the genitals and is a personality-altering drug, it causes drowsiness, lack of concentration and in some cases acute paranoia – in fact it's as dangerous a drug as heroin. And do not forget that passive smoking is at least as harmful – if not more so – than active smoking.'

Gatey could not help thinking of her brother's itching genitals. 'Oh piss off Evidence!' she said crossly, and then wished she hadn't because, after all, she was a guest in his house and besides, she wanted his help where their grandmother, and possibly their father too, were concerned.

'Oh sorry,' she said, jumping up and flinging her arms round her brother's neck to give him a big kiss. 'I promise to try not to smoke any more.' As she spoke she momentarily believed what she was saying.

'And it makes you smell,' said Evidence, receiving Gatey's kiss stiffly and wrinkling up his nose again.

Gatey glanced at her brother, amazed, and almost lit

up another cigarette in defiance. He was very good-looking, she thought, but it was a pity he was so buttoned-up and priggish. It rather spoilt the effect. In some ways he was extraordinarily like their father but in others he might just as well have landed from the moon as be born to her parents. She thought that Milly might have loosened him up a bit but he hardly seemed to have changed at all since they had been together.

Evidence mostly reminded Gatey of their father when he had an obsession, the only difference being that Frederick's obsessions had all been vaguely more attractive than any of Evidence's. She could hardly imagine her father becoming so concerned about smoking, he was more likely to go for horses or the metaphysical poets or even the migratory habits of the red-throated pipit. She could remember them all and almost tell the story of her childhood by them. The red-throated pipit had had its day during the summer of her eighth birthday – and after that it had been Viking history and then back to the metaphysical poets. There never seemed to be any rhyme or reason for these extraordinary enthusiasms which, when you came to think about it, didn't seem to have done Frederick much good, either.

'At least your crazes keep you clean in body and mind I suppose,' Gatey grinned at Evidence. 'Do you remember being carted all the way to Scotland on the day we were meant to be going back to school, to look for a red-throated pipit?'

Evidence pretended not to hear and turned instead to Milly to make some remark about tea. Gatey wondered how on earth she was going to approach him. His ability to cut out what he didn't want to know was sometimes uncanny, as was his ability to avoid confrontation of any kind and to ward off inconvenient conversations.

She decided to wait until after they had eaten before saying anything, but as soon as they had finished tea, and while Milly and she were still washing up Evidence turned on the television and settled into an armchair. In the end Milly came to the rescue.

'Evidence,' she said, 'I think Gatey's got something she wants to talk to you about. That's why she's come here.'

Evidence went on watching television. 'Sh . . .' he said, 'I can't hear what they're saying if you talk.'

'That rubbish isn't worth hearing anyway,'said Gatey angrily. She wished she could keep her cool, but how did you cope with someone like her brother? Suddenly she jumped up and went and stood between him and the television; she put her hands on her hips and bent down towards him, almost shouting, 'Dad is probably dying. Aren't you more interested in that?'

'Oh Gatey,' said Evidence languidly, 'if you've got something to say, please say it quietly.' But Gatey detected a hint of a reaction behind the supercilious manner. She whipped round, switched off the television and turned back to face Evidence and drive home her advantage.

'Please,' she said earnestly, 'please help me. At least read this horrible letter from Granny.'

The last thing Evidence wanted was to have his grandmother brought into the matter, but he was moved by the sight of his sister standing there in front of him with her silly, cropped hair and all those silly earrings, by her sense of urgency and by the innocence of her expression. Poor little Gatey, he thought.

'Give us the letter then,' he said.

When he had read it, he simply said, 'I wouldn't do anything about it if I were you. She's only trying to get your attention.'

'But what about Dad – poor Dad? He might need us; we must find out where he is.'

'He's never needed us before,' Evidence said coldly. 'He's done nothing but make us all miserable, he's shown no responsibility towards his family whatsoever and he's cut himself off from us. We have absolutely no obligation towards him at all.'

Milly kept quiet.

'Oh Evidence,' Gatey said almost in a whisper. 'You need to go and see somebody.'

'See somebody? What about?' Evidence livened up.

'Oh, you know, a psycho-something – a nut doctor – somebody to sort you out.' She was out of control again.

If Gatey really wanted to trace their father, which Evidence thought was a very bad idea indeed, he suggested that she ring Lady Field quite simply to ask her what she meant by the mysterious postscript in her letter. She would have to answer. There was certainly no point in going to see her as she was bound to be unpleasant and it would involve running endless, unnecessary errands. Evidence was still fuming about Milly and the tin of cat food.

Later that evening Gatey did summon up her courage and ring her grandmother's number, but not without begging Evidence to let her light a cigarette first. For all his pomposity, he was not a sadist and as he could see that Gatey's hand was shaking he agreed, but of course added a little homily about the dangers of nicotine.

'Oh go back to your mania about French eating apples, for God's sake,' said Gatey. Last time she had seen her brother she had been bored stiff by his banging on and on about Golden Delicious – a rather dated obsession, she thought at the time, as most people

74

seemed already to have taken on board the horrors of those big, green apples in a vague, uninterested sort of way.

'How very selfish of you to ring so late, dear,' were Lady Field's first words. 'I don't have the energy of you young people and am about to go to bed.' It was only nine o'clock and Gatey knew perfectly well that Lady Field was a creature of habit and that although she was getting on in years she never went to bed before ten o'clock. In fact, she always went to bed immediately after the ten o'clock news headlines.

'I want to know where my father is,' Gatey blurted out.

'Now why should I have the slightest idea about that?' said Lady Field. 'You are a silly girl. I sit here alone day in and day out and no one bothers about me – in fact none of you would mind if I was run over by a bus tomorrow – and then you suddenly ring me up, out of the blue, much too late at night to ask me a ridiculous question like that! How on earth should I know where your father is? As far as I'm concerned, he's never faced up to his responsibilities, he's abandoned his family and that is that. I should hardly think that after the way he treated all of you, you would want to know where he was anyway. I must say that I never want to see him again. I mean, Mrs Moffat's son-in-law looks in on her every evening on his way home from work just to see if she's all right, and he comes round at weekends to do odd jobs for her. Now what did your father ever do for me, I should like to know? All he ever did was to drink himself silly and talk a lot of rot. A useless man. Psychopathic, I should say . . .'

Gatey was so furious that she slammed down the telephone without saying a word. Then she burst into tears.

Evidence felt sorry for her, but finding it hard to be demonstrative himself, he was glad to see Milly put her arms round her. No wonder he chose to distance himself from his family, he thought; whenever he had any contact with them there was bound to be trouble.

Sometimes the very word 'family' made Evidence feel tense all over and shrink inside, so that when Milly began to talk of having babies he froze and would come up with any excuse for putting it off for a little longer. He felt slightly sick at the thought of all the personal closeness and intimacy that babies would be bound to bring with them and then, as they grew into children, they would surely remind him of his own childhood, the thought of which always discountenanced him. Very occasionally he imagined having one daughter, who would grow up to be exactly like Milly and who would be a comfort to him in his old age. But perhaps that one daughter would take part of Milly from him and that was an idea which he could not tolerate, since Milly was his all.

'Don't cry, Gatey,' said Milly, 'just think of her as a pathetic, rather unhappy, old woman. She's just taking her bitterness out on you, but she can't really hurt you, you know she can't.'

'But she can, she can,' wailed Gatey.

'No,' said Milly 'she can't. You will have to go and see her if you want to find out what – if anything – she meant about your father, but we won't let you go alone, will we Evidence?' She turned and looked sternly at her husband. 'You'll go with her, won't you?' she added firmly.

Evidence who used to smoke, suddenly badly wanted a cigarette. He pushed his hands deep into his trouser pockets, hunched up his shoulders and paced up and down the small sitting-room like a caged lion, head bent, scowling at the floor, reciting silently to himself his litany of tobacco related disorders.

'You look like you used to look when you were giving up smoking,' said Milly to Evidence with a laugh.

'Have a Golden Delicious instead,' said Gatey, pulling herself together.

'Oh do shut up both of you!' Evidence spoke with unusual feeling.

Gatey broke away from Milly's embrace and went over to her brother. She took him by the arm to stop his pacing and said, 'Come on Evidence, you're as neurotic as the rest of us – look at the way you pace up and down at the mere mention of Granny. Milly's quite right, Granny can't do us any harm. She's just a pathetic old bag. Let's just go up there tomorrow evening without warning her – you and me. You'll have to come to stop me from strangling the old witch. You see, if you come, it'll be all calm and civilised, which is what you like, and we'll just ask her what she knows and go away again. And you won't have to do anything about Dad if we find him, I promise. It's me who wants to see him.'

'OK,' he said, 'just this once, for you Gates.' A rare smile lit his handsome features. 'But I may need to smoke,' he added.

'Oh, no, Evidence, please don't do that,' Milly almost screamed as she rushed forward and grabbed him by his free arm.

Gatey was laughing and crying and thanking Evidence and saying how wonderful he was and hugging him, and Milly was clutching his arm and reminding him of all the awful things that tobacco would do to him, and Evidence was longing to get away from both of them and wondering quite how it was that things had managed to get so out of control when he remembered his grandmother and her evil genius. It was, of course, all due to her.

'Right,' he said, shaking himself free of them both, 'will you two leave me alone? Let's sit down quietly now and watch the television, then tomorrow, Gatey, I will come back from work and pick you up and we'll go straight round and see Granny, but let's not talk about it any more now.'

Gatey obediently turned the television back on and she and Milly sat down, but Evidence plunged his hands deep into his pockets and resumed his pacing.

VI

In the village shop people were saying that Wilf Wap-shott's van was always to be seen parked outside the Old Rectory these days. Perhaps he was sweet on the new housekeeper up there – not that she could be expected to stay for long – no one ever did. Then someone suggested that if she was sweet on Wilf things might be different this time. She seemed a quiet sort of person, nice enough, not that anyone could say a lot since no one had had much to do with her. Someone else suggested that she had a daughter who'd been down to visit who looked like some sort of drug addict. Rumours were rife, too, about Hardcastle, whom no one liked at all and who would be lucky if he could keep a housekeeper for a twelvemonth.

Sylvia wasn't properly aware of the rumours, but she did vaguely wonder if anyone had noticed quite how often Wilf's van was there. She had begun to be really pleased to see him, even to look forward to his visits, which were now no longer tied to mending things in the Old Rectory. She had found a friend and it gave her pleasure to sit for hours chatting to Wilf and to listen to him talking about his life. There was something attractive about his self-deprecatory manner and the ease with which he talked. Sometimes he had tea with her and once she baked a cake and gave it to him to take home for the weekend.

Wilf told her that knowing she was there to talk to had changed his life.

'Steady on,' she said. Then she thought that what she should have said was that having him there had changed her life, too. She asked herself what it was about him that she liked so much for, despite his easy manner, she sometimes noticed a hooded look come over him, then it crossed her mind to wonder if she could really trust him, and there seemed to be a coldness about him as he withdrew into himself.

What with Wilf and Hardcastle, Sylvia's life had suddenly become a great deal less lonely, but where Wilf was a consolation, Hardcastle was a menace. There was no doubt at all in Sylvia's mind that Hardcastle had developed a drunken crush on her, which meant that he was forever begging her to come and sit with him and that he had begun to confide in her all his inadequacies and miseries. This she found quite unpleasing, but despite everything she could not but feel sorry for him; knowing him to be lonely she felt an obligation to listen. But listening to Hardcastle was one thing, getting away from him was quite another. It was sometimes so difficult for Sylvia to break away and to get back to her side of the house, which she had come to regard as a blessed haven despite its gloomy appearance, that she occasionally made up her mind to harden her heart and to refuse ever to sit down in his kitchen again.

But that was easier said than done and, in a way, Sylvia felt even sorrier for Hardcastle now that she had found herself a friend in Wilf. A further problem derived from the fact that sometimes when Sylvia did get away, Hardcastle would follow her into her side of the house and ask if he might sit down and talk to her for a few minutes.

'You're not too busy, are you?' he'd ask. 'If you are, just leave it till tomorrow. It'll keep. I won't mind.' He seemed to be sublimely unaware of the fact that she might be busy on her own account, or just wish to be alone, and that her entire life was not devoted to his comfort.

He was sitting one day at her kitchen table, with a glass of whisky he had brought through from next door, his eyes already out of focus at just on six o'clock when he suddenly said in slurred tones, 'Jocelyn's coming. Did I tell you? You'll see how beautiful she is.'

Sylvia was amazed and suddenly, since her curiosity was aroused, less anxious to be rid of Hardcastle despite his drunkenness. She wondered what it might be that had tempted the beautiful Jocelyn to call on her father at last.

It turned out that Lady Field's visit, which was drawing unpleasantly close, would coincide with Jocelyn's and that, Sylvia thought, was rather a pity since she couldn't help being nosy and she was quite looking forward to studying Jocelyn. Lady Field would certainly be a hindrance.

'How long will Jocelyn be here?' Sylvia wanted to know.

'She'll stay a week,' Hardcastle replied. 'At least a week, I should think.' He stood up slowly and unsteadily and very carefully and, with immense concentration, picked up his empty glass. 'I'll have to go,' he mumbled, 'I've got a sermon to write for Sunday.'

And a glass to refill, Sylvia thought. She wondered what on earth the sermon would be like, but not for long, as she felt that she already knew all she ever wanted to know about drunken sermons.

'I thank God every day for my sufferings,' Hardcastle said as he left the room. But he didn't enunciate the word 'sufferings' very well.

'Oh, go away!' said Sylvia to herself, wriggling her shoulders in disgust and irritation as he closed the door behind him. At least Frederick had never been sanctimonious.

When Wilf came round the next day she told him about Jocelyn and about how drunk Hardcastle had been. She no longer allowed loyalty to her employer to come between herself and Wilf.

In fact, Wilf wasn't at all surprised by any of it. It was pretty well known around the village that Hardcastle put it away quite heavily. Some of the earlier housekeepers had been far less discreet than Sylvia. Wilf wouldn't say a word. He didn't gossip. Never had. In any case, he didn't see many of the people in the village, not to talk to.

'I expect they'll soon have something to say about your van always being parked here,' Sylvia said with a smile.

'You can't stop people thinking what they want to think and saying what they want to say,' Wilf remarked, 'especially in a village like this.'

Now that Sylvia was growing so fond of Wilf and devoting so much of her time and imagination to him, she was beginning to dread the arrival of her mother even more than usual. She didn't want to ban Wilf from her kitchen, for one thing she realised that she would miss him if he didn't come, but she was terrified of how her mother would treat him. The last thing she wanted was for Wilf to be offended. Lady Field was nothing if not a snob who would consider Wilf beneath her and, furthermore, Sylvia knew full well that if her mother so much as suspected the closeness of the friendship, she would do her utmost to put a spoke in the wheels. She wouldn't, for instance, hesitate for one moment to discuss Sylvia in the most dismissive and undermining terms in front of her, as though she weren't in the room. She would also be quite capable of engineering to be alone with Wilf so as to entice him into her web, where she would confidingly explain what an inadequate and pathetic person or what a hard-hearted and selfish person Sylvia was. The thought of the variety of different possibilities – all of which were familiar to her – made Sylvia feel slightly sick.

The best thing that she could do was to warn Wilf about her mother, but she even found this a little difficult as she thought it might shock him to hear her talk about her mother in disparaging tones.

But Wilf wasn't in the least bit shocked, merely remarking that Lady Field would probably look down her nose at him for being just an ordinary working man. He'd come across her sort.

Sylvia rather doubted that anyone who had not met Lady Field could begin to know her sort. She was unique.

Jocelyn had a lampshade shop in Fulham and above the shop she had a flat. All this had been provided for her by her father who, she knew, would give her anything she asked for. At first the lampshade shop had seemed a brilliant idea and Jocelyn who was indeed very beautiful and who mixed with media people, decadent aristocrats and drifters, had fondly imagined herself as the purveyor of lampshades to the rich and famous. True to say, a duchess had once come into the shop and so had a film star, whose name she couldn't remember, but neither of them had bought anything, not even one of her ludicrously expensive, pink silk affairs.

To begin with Jocelyn had been fantastically enthusiastic about the whole venture, but lately things had started to go rather wrong. Business was terribly slack and Jocelyn was even wondering just how long she could sustain an interest in lampshades. She should have had a different kind of shop really because, after all, there was only so much to be done with a lampshade. So few people came into the shop these days that it hardly seemed worth her while to open it up in the mornings. She had stopped setting her alarm a long time ago now and usually slept until nearly midday. She wasn't a junkie, she knew that because she could drop the habit – if it was a habit – any time she chose. She just didn't really want to. She wasn't doing anyone any harm.

Then the bills started to come in and Jocelyn didn't bother to pay them. Often she didn't even bother to open them. Then suddenly one day she began to be rather afraid and then she realised that she would probably have to go and see her father who would have to pay the bills for her. She hoped he would do it without asking any awkward questions. One other possibility was a rich young lord she knew who might pay some of the bills if she slept with him, but she couldn't really be bothered to get involved, although she could see that it might eventually have to come to that. On the whole she would rather her father paid. For one thing he deserved to pay. She hated her father somehow, but in what she recognised as a very peculiar, twisted sort of way, she also sometimes kind of loved him. But above all she preferred not to have to see him very often, partly because of his abominably claustrophobic, clammy love for her and partly because of all the memories of her childhood which his presence evoked. Memories which she did not really have any desire to confront.

Jocelyn's boyfriend of the moment was a languid junkie called Jason. He was a junkie and Jocelyn sort of thought that he needed her and that she could help him in a way. He certainly needed some kind of help which he wasn't getting. But sometimes Jocelyn found his total inertia and his obsession with himself and death and suicide so undermining that she felt she would have to stop seeing him whether he needed her nor not. She wondered about taking him with her to see her father and decided that it would be a good idea. For one thing he would somehow stand between her and her father and, for another, it might cheer him up to get out of London.

She hated the idea of ringing her father to announce her arrival because she dreaded the emotional response and the slurred, drunken voice, so she thought instead of writing him a note, but the idea of having to go out and buy a stamp put her off that. She supposed that there just might be a stamp in the shop but she seemed to remember that she had run out long ago and she hadn't bothered to buy any more.

When she eventually got round to ringing her father she was quite surprised to hear him singing the praises of his new housekeeper, Sylvia Something-or-other. Well that was a good thing in itself. He usually had the most awful women to work for him and they usually left almost as soon as they had arrived. In fact he had so much to say about this Sylvia that she didn't feel herself to be quite so swamped as usual by his emotions, although his voice did falter a little when she announced that she would be bringing Jason with her.

'He's awfully nice, I'm sure you'll like him,' she heard herself lying, and as she spoke she wondered why on earth she had bothered.

When it came to the point Jason didn't seem to want to get out of London at all. Jocelyn supposed that he was afraid of being too far away from his suppliers; Jason, she thought, was a loser. If he wouldn't come she might need someone else to take his place and so she began to wonder about the rich young lord. That'd be quite good because then they could go down in his car. Perhaps, she thought, she could get her father to give her a car some time, but it might have to wait until all these horrid bills were settled. She hadn't even added them all up, but there were quite a few and some were for several thousands of pounds.

The rich young lord was delighted at the prospect of driving Jocelyn down to stay with her father – he thought he was in with a chance, but, unfortunately for him he wrote his very expensive car off in a head-on crash with a lorry the day before they were due to go. He was lucky to get out alive, but was taken to hospital to be treated for shock and bruising, leaving Jocelyn to travel alone by train.

Jocelyn felt rather shaky on the morning she was due to leave. She found it really difficult to get out of bed before one o'clock and, as she stuffed all the awful bills together with a couple of silk shirts into a beautiful leather holdall, she was assaulted by violent waves of nausea. She felt depressed and irritable and wished she could stay in London.

She only just caught the train and as it moved out of the station she fell into a seat beside a neatly-dressed, nice-looking elderly lady.

'Just in time!' the neatly-dressed lady said brightly.

'Oh my God,' thought Jocelyn as she stretched,

arched her back and ran her long fingers through a mane of thick, black curly hair, 'I can't cope with bright conversation at the moment.' She grunted a non-committal reply without even glancing at her neighbour.

The old lady looked at Jocelyn long and hard and thought what a beautiful girl she was, but a bit drawn. She felt that she would like to engage her in conversation but that it might prove tricky, so she decided to let her settle a bit before making any further attempt.

About ten minutes later Jocelyn got up to fetch some coffee from the buffet. Neatly-dressed meanwhile inspected the two people sitting opposite her – a grumpy, beige middle-aged man and his equally grumpy wife, who sat with pursed lips looking straight ahead, her head framed in turquoise angora, her hands folded on her lap – and decided that they would be no fun to talk to. She would wait for the beautiful girl to come back. Soon the beautiful girl came lurching down the corridor carrying a giant beaker of British Rail coffee; heads turned to watch her pass as she clasped the backs of seats with long, white, bony hands and swayed from side to side. She was tall and rather foreign-looking with masses of hair – very striking indeed.

'Are you going far?' asked Neatly-dressed as Jocelyn settled down beside her again.

'Battle,' said Jocelyn brusquely, concentrating on lifting the brimming beaker of coffee to her lips.

'Now isn't that strange?' said Neatly-dressed. 'What a coincidence! That's just where I'm going, too.'

Jocelyn could hardly see that it was much of a coincidence that two people travelling on the same train should be heading for the same destination, but she said nothing.

Just as Jocelyn was about to take a sip from her coffee the train gave an enormous, unexpected jolt and the beaker went flying out of her hand; the coffee went everywhere, it swam across the table in front of her to be partly absorbed by a carefully folded copy of the *Daily Mail* belonging to Grumpy-beige, and it trickled down over the edge and fell in a steady stream on to Neatly-dressed's burgundy, plastic handbag.

At this point Jocelyn was obliged to do something, if only to apologise. Neatly-dressed leapt to the occasion and miraculously produced an enormous wad of paper handkerchiefs from her sticky burgundy handbag. Grumpy said nothing, but clicked his tongue and moved the sodden *Daily Mail* a few inches towards him, thus spreading the mess even further across the table. Mrs Grumpy remained immobile, lips forever pursed. None of it was any of her business. She had no need to stir.

Jocelyn flapped her hands and did nothing but keep apologising, while Neatly-dressed somehow managed to restore some semblance of order. Jocelyn could not but be grateful, especially in view of the hostility aimed at her from the other side of the table, and in her gratitude she allowed herself to be drawn into conversation with Neatly-dressed – or at least to listen to what turned out to be a loud monologue.

'So you are going to Battle,' said Neatly-dressed, once everything was calm again. 'I haven't been to that part of the country before myself, but I'm going to see my daughter who has just moved down there. Personally, I've never been particularly attracted to that part of England. I live in Manchester myself, and my heart has always been in the North-West. The people up there are so much nicer than they are down south. More warm-hearted I should say, whereas down here it's all self and money. I mean, look at the young people these days – all of them out of work, all living on the dole, taking everything from the State and giving nothing in return. I should know, my granddaughter's one of them. Honestly, I sometimes feel quite ashamed on her behalf. It's not as if she wasn't brought up to know better – not that her parents were very good examples really; my daughter, for instance – that's the one I'm going to see – she's very selfish herself. Yes, I'd say she's totally self-absorbed. Exactly like her father of course. I mean, exactly. My dear,' she pushed her face into Jocelyn's, 'I hope you never have to go through what I went through with my late husband – and I never was thanked for it. Not one word of thanks did I ever get.'

Despite herself, Jocelyn was beginning to be quite mesmerised. It required no effort on her part to listen to this monologue, but she was beginning to wonder just how long it could go on for, and now even the couple opposite were beginning to show some interest.

'Then my daughter went and married a drunk; of course, I knew that wouldn't work out, but would she listen to me? Oh no. But then they never do, do they?' Lady Field glanced round at her audience. Grumpy was looking in her direction and beginning to smirk and nod and even Mrs Grumpy's lips seemed to be pursed with greater intensity than before.

'They're never interested in anything that anyone wiser or older than themselves has to say. Well of course it all broke up, which was for the better, except that it left my daughter without a penny – and just at a time when she might have been thinking of helping out her elderly mother. Mind you, as I say, my daughter's quite a selfish person and not very strong in many ways, even quite a weak person I should say . . .'

Grumpy and Mrs Grumpy were clearly warming to the theme; Grumpy even intervened with some disagreeable remark of his own about the selfishness of the younger generation, while Mrs Grumpy nodded in approval.

'They should never have abolished military service in my opinion,' he said.

Lady Field gave him a cursory glance and continued unhaltingly with her own flow of consciousness. 'I never thought the day would come when my daughter would stoop to become a domestic servant,' her loud voice ground on. 'After all, her father was knighted – I well remember the day we went to the Palace – oh, it was some years ago now. "I'm sure it is you who really deserve this award," was what the Queen said to me. "You are so very kind, ma'am" was what I replied . . .' She interrupted herself to lean across the table and explain to the Grumpies that when speaking to the Queen, it was correct to address her as 'ma'am'.

Jocelyn was beginning to think that the woman was quite crazy, banging on like that about the Queen, and other people were beginning to turn round and stare.

'Her Majesty was dressed in lemon yellow on that occasion,' Lady Field went on, 'a colour in which she always looks well, but not a colour I would necessarily choose myself; and now, after all that, and Her Majesty having bothered to put on the lemon yellow and one thing and another, there's my daughter, sunk into oblivion and working as a domestic servant.' All of a sudden Lady Field began to feel that the picture she was giving of her daughter might somehow demean her in the eyes of her audience, so she began to change tack ever so slightly.

'Well, I say "domestic servant", but of course that's only a manner of speaking. In fact she's acting as housekeeper to a charming, very well-to-do widower. I think you might say that she's rather more than a housekeeper really, you know, she sits with him and keeps him company . . . a kind of companion, you could say . . .'

At this point Jocelyn did a double take. 'What's the village called where she lives?' she asked.

Lady Field told her.

'Yeah,' said Jocelyn, 'I thought so.' But Lady Field didn't seem to notice.

'I suppose it is a coincidence us both going to Battle after all,' Jocelyn mused, but Lady Field wasn't interested in that now, she was hell-bent on restoring her own reputation which she alone had damaged.

'If you want to know,' she was saying, 'I think he is a remarkably lucky man to have my daughter there; she is an extremely good cook and that's something which she's learnt from her mother, although I say it as shouldn't. Well, I don't in fact see why I shouldn't say it. Anyway, for all I know there may be more to the relationship than that, after all, Sylvia's not a bad-looking woman – or she wouldn't be if she made a bit of an effort – well, we shall see, there may be wedding bells yet. It would be a good thing for Sylvia, what with all his money and with what I am told is an extremely nice house . . .'

Jocelyn just longed for the woman to shut up. She had looked round to see if there was an empty seat she could move to but the train was packed and there was nothing to be done but to sit it out. She decided to shut her eyes and try – or if not try, at least pretend – to go to sleep. She was absolutely not prepared to reveal her identity at the moment, that would have to come later, and very embarrassing it would prove to be; or perhaps this woman was so insensitive that the whole episode would leave her quite untouched. Jocelyn wondered about that as she closed her eyes and settled into her corner, leaving the Grumpies to deal with the never-ending flow of chatter.

There was no question of Jocelyn falling asleep though, not only because she had begun to feel very angry. If this Sylvia person had some kind of a hold on her father it might be very much more difficult than she had imagined persuading him to pay her bills. She usually had very little trouble, but it sounded as though things had rather changed; her father himself had been full of this housekeeper when she spoke to him on the telephone. She began to feel rather panicky and to think of the house – her home, which no one, she felt, had the right to touch – and of her father whom she hated but whom, she also felt, no one had the right to touch. She wished she hadn't come, she wished that this Sylvia person had never been born – what right had she to come and have designs on their home – on them? Jocelyn already hated her.

The voice beside her ground on and on, but eventually Jocelyn managed to blot it out a bit and even to doze a little.

At Battle station Sylvia waited nervously for the train. She felt that with the arrival of her mother she would be losing her freedom and, furthermore, in some unavoidable and inexplicable way, be reduced to the status of a child again. She was nervous about the fact that Jocelyn was on the same train as her mother and Hardcastle had asked her to meet his daughter because he himself would not be able to leave work on time as he had an important client to see that afternoon. Sylvia was embarrassed by the thought of taking Jocelyn and Lady Field home together. She would have liked to have been able to feel the ground before the two met. Her mother would probably say a lot of dreadfully embarrassing things and Sylvia could just imagine herself behind the wheel, tense and careful, like a girl who had only just passed her test.

She told herself she was being silly because, after all, what was Jocelyn to her? And she had to suppose that, however awful her mother might be, people on the whole did not judge one by one's mother.

Sylvia was in good time, waiting on the platform so as to be able to help Lady Field with her suitcase. She would, she felt sure, be able to recognise Jocelyn easily from photographs she had seen of her.

The train was twenty minutes late and it was raining. Sylvia was pacing up and down, feeling herself grow more tense all the time. There was something niggling at the back of her mind and she wasn't quite sure what to think of it. Gatey had telephoned just before she left for the station and Sylvia couldn't really make out what it was all about, but a warning note had rung in her mind. Gatey seemed to be in Manchester with Evidence and they were planning to go and see their grandmother that evening on some mysterious mission about which Gatey refused to come clean. She was absolutely furious when she discovered that Lady Field was on her way to Sussex where she planned to stay for at least ten days.

Sylvia was left with the uncomfortable feeling that Gatey had really just been trying to sound her out and find out if she knew something – she had no idea what, and neither could she imagine what sort of thing it might be. It was particularly odd that Evidence had apparently agreed to accompany Gatey on this mission. It was very unlike him to allow himself to become involved in any sort of family machinations. Sylvia couldn't make it out at all.

The train came roaring into the station and Sylvia began to run up and down the platform frantically looking for her mother. A tall, dark, beautiful girl jumped off the train even before it had stopped and brushed past Sylvia on her way to the exit. Sylvia recognised her as Jocelyn, but dared not run after her for fear of leaving her mother to fend for herself with her suitcase; then she saw Lady Field struggling down from the train, old now and afraid of falling. She rushed to help her and as they walked slowly towards the exit, Sylvia was able to explain that she had also to find Jocelyn Hardcastle.

Jocelyn was standing just outside the station, looking anxiously to right and left for any sign of her father, when Sylvia introduced herself. She was greeted by Jocelyn with a supercilious 'Hi,' and then, 'I thought my father would be here to meet me.'

Sylvia introduced her mother and Jocelyn said coldly, 'We've already met – on the train – remember?' and gave Lady Field the coldest and most sarcastic look she had ever given anyone, then she just turned away and said, 'So which car?'

Sylvia was puzzled by Jocelyn's bad manners and found herself being embarrassed by her, rather than by her mother, for a change. Lady Field, who had not appeared in the least little bit discountenanced by meeting Jocelyn, was being quite meek and mild for once, hoping that Sylvia hadn't been cold while she waited and apologising for the train being late. Sylvia wondered, as she did whenever her mother behaved normally, whether she hadn't been being inordinately unfair to her, until then.

'I'm so sorry, darling, that you should have had to wait so long in the rain. What a nuisance for you, but, I must say, it is lovely to be here. Lovely for me.'

Sylvia had momentarily to concentrate on all the bad things her mother had done to her which had made her feel the way she did, otherwise she would have been so overwhelmed with guilt that her belief in her own integrity would have been shattered.

'Mummy, I'm so glad you're here,' she said, almost sincerely.

Jocelyn climbed into the back of Sylvia's old red Volkswagen without saying a word. There wasn't a great deal of room for her very long legs and she was infuriated by the two silly women in the front. How dared that bloody Sylvia, who looked so sweet and meek and mild, have designs on her father!

VII

When Gatey rang her mother it was really just to sound her out and to find out if Lady Field had said anything to her about Frederick, but Sylvia had sounded so baffled on the telephone that Gatey was convinced of her ignorance of the whole matter. The revelation that Sylvia was about to leave the house to go and collect Lady Field from the station enraged her. She vaguely remembered that her mother had mentioned some such plan, but she had no idea when it was for and she was incensed that her grandmother had not bothered to mention it on the telephone the night before.

So there was Gatey, in Manchester, having managed to persuade Evidence to come to her assistance, all ready to beard the lion in her den that very evening and the lion wasn't there any more – and wouldn't be there for a little while, by which time Evidence might have changed his mind and decided that the whole thing was a storm in a teacup. Gatey anyway would have to get back to London to sign on and in any case she couldn't just hang around in Manchester for ever. She had no idea what to do next. Evidence would be back from work presently and expecting to go straight over to their grandmother's house.

Over the last few days Gatey had worked herself into a lather of concern about her father. She knew that to a certain extent Evidence was right in that it was no one's fault but Frederick's that he had disappeared, and she could even understand why Evidence wanted nothing to do with him, but she could not feel the same way herself. She had absolutely no idea how one set about looking for missing persons and didn't really suppose that the police would be much help. She had a vague idea anyway that if you were over the age of consent, or something, you had a perfect right to disappear, if that was what you wanted.

But the problem, as she saw it, was the fact that if, having disappeared, you wanted to reappear and all your family had dispersed, you would be done for. This was the idea which haunted her. She even thought of ringing the Samaritans. Weren't they the people you were supposed to turn to when all else failed? But how could they, for all their good will, whistle her father out of nowhere? Then she began to think about suicide and she got it into her head that if Frederick was as desperate as she had begun to imagine he might be, he could have reached the point of no return himself.

'Oh, don't say that,' said Milly.

'I could always ring Granny later at Mum's,' Gatey said.

'That wouldn't help much, though, if she behaved as she did last night,' Milly said. 'I mean she wasn't exactly helpful, was she?'

'Perhaps Evidence would try,' Gatey wondered. 'After all, he did agree to come and see her.'

'Here he comes,' said Milly. She had heard his key in the front door.

'Right,' said Evidence, coming into the kitchen, 'are you ready, Gatey? We're off.' His face was set hard in an expression of humourless distaste. 'If we're going, let's get it over with.'

'We can't,' said Gatey. 'She's not there.'

Evidence's hard outward exterior was something at which he had been working for years, to protect himself first of all from any emotions he might feel about his family and then to protect himself from any emotion at all. But underneath – and not even very far underneath – he knew himself to be quite as vulnerable as the next man. He knew because he knew how he felt about Milly, although he never allowed himself to tell her quite how much he needed her and relied on her, nor even quite how much he loved her. If he told her all that it would leave him defenceless. He also knew that in a different sort of way he loved Gatey. Somehow, from earliest youth, she had always possessed the power to move him.

The result of all this was that since the scene of the evening before a lot of latent emotion had been stirred up in Evidence and he had been struggling all day to maintain the hard veneer. He really had no desire at all to see his father. The very idea of it filled him with horror, and neither could he possibly imagine introducing Milly to him. He had a sort of ridiculous fear, only half-admitted, even to himself, that were she to be confronted with the drunken failure of Frederick, she would give a sideways glance at Evidence and be off.

At the same time, despite the strength of his own personal stand against his father, somewhere in the corner of his heart he wanted to know that Frederick was all right. This was partly what had made him agree with Gatey to go and see their grandmother. Perhaps there was too a faint hope that it would all turn out to have been a dreadful nightmare and that Frederick would be a reformed character, urbane and charming and witty and clever, as he had been years ago in his best moments before the liquor had taken such a stranglehold.

Evidence came back that evening unusually keyed up and ready to face the problem ahead and so when he learned that his grandmother had gone to Sussex he was more than ready to go ahead and ring her there.

Gatey was worried that by doing that they might upset their mother, but having got himself into a mood to act, there was no holding Evidence. He couldn't really see that their mother needed protecting, for one thing, and, for another, it was absolutely unthinkable that Lady Field could spend one day – let alone ten – with her daughter without telling her of any unpleasant piece of news she might have in store.

It was normal for Lady Field to choose her moment with care. If she had anything worth saying, she would be sure to say it at the most awkward moment for everyone or, as she saw it, the moment when she was most likely to be heeded. She had indeed something interesting to tell Sylvia, but she hadn't yet decided how or when to tell her, so she was particularly disconcerted to be telephoned about it by Evidence so soon after her arrival in Sussex.

Sylvia was made to feel rather nervous about the whole thing. Evidence hardly ever telephoned and on this occasion he was quite curt and seemed to be in a terrible hurry to speak to his grandmother and then when Lady Field was called to the telephone she looked immensely put out. For once Sylvia decided that it would not really be beneath her to eavesdrop, but, most unfortunately, just as Lady Field began to speak Percy Hardcastle appeared at Sylvia's kitchen door, bleary-eyed and swaying, to ask her to bring her mother to have a glass of sherry and to meet Jocelyn.

The last thing Sylvia wanted to do was to take her mother to meet Jocelyn. She felt that she had seen quite enough of her for one day on the journey back from the station.

'Wouldn't Jocelyn prefer to spend this first evening with you?' she suggested hopefully.

'Not at all,' said Hardcastle, 'she'd love to meet you.'

Considering Hardcastle's condition, Sylvia thought that that might well be true and as he was very insistent and went on badgering her, she eventually had no alternative but to agree.

Meanwhile, Lady Field had finished her conversation with Evidence without Sylvia having been able to hear any of it, which was just as well because it meant that Lady Field still had that useful little piece of information up her sleeve, to be produced at a suitable moment. Unfortunately, she had told Evidence what he wanted to know over the telephone. She had never meant to do that, but it was awkward being in Sylvia's kitchen with that man at the door and all she had really wanted to do was to get rid of her grandson. Besides, she, like Sylvia, had been quite disconcerted at hearing Evidence's voice down the line. Gatey she could have coped with, she thought.

When Evidence had finished talking to his grand-mother he was a little surprised and somewhat put out to find that his hands were shaking. It was ridiculous the effect his family had on him. No wonder he usually tried to avoid having any dealings with them.

'So what did she say?' Gatey was dying to know.

God Almighty! Evidence wanted a cigarette. 'I'll tell you in a minute,' he said and walked stiffly to the sideboard and took out a bottle of gin. 'Have we got anything to mix with this?' he waved the bottle in Milly's direction.

'Is it as bad as that?' Milly asked with a smile. She was surprised to see Evidence taking a drink. Reaction to his father's alcoholism was, she supposed, what had made her husband a bit of a prig and he very rarely drank at all. Perhaps he was afraid of following Frederick down the slippery slope.

'Well, if you're having a drink let's all have one,' said Gatey, 'and then we'll be ready to hear the worst.'

They found a bottle of Martini at the back of the sideboard and mixed themselves some drinks.

Then Evidence said, 'Well, Gatey, I've found out what you wanted to know. But I've no idea what you think you're going to do about it.' He paused. Suddenly he felt rather embarrassed and didn't really know how to go on. What should he say?

'Perhaps it's not true,' he said, grasping at straws, 'but she says she saw him here, in Manchester, not long ago – outside Boot's or W.H. Smith or somewhere like that.'

'So what did he say – and how was he?' Gatey wanted to know.

'She didn't talk to him, but she says she knows it was him, although he had changed a lot. He looked awful.'

'Awful – how?' Gatey demanded. 'And why didn't she talk to him – the bitch?'

'Oh, Gatey,' said Evidence, 'I don't suppose it would have helped. And do you really think that he would have wanted to talk to her – especially in the condition he was in?'

Gatey wanted to know everything, but Evidence had only talked to his grandmother for such a short time that there was not really all that much he could say.

Their father apparently looked like an old tramp, a real down-and-out, and filthy dirty too.

Gatey burst into tears. It was all too awful, she couldn't bear it. What was she to do, and how was she to find him? Was he still in Manchester? How did you set about tracing tramps and why hadn't her horrible grandmother found out at least where Frederick was living?

Milly had put down her drink and gone to put her arms round Gatey.

'Don't worry,' she said. 'I'm sure we'll be able to find him somehow.' Not that she really had any confidence in what she was saying.

'I'm afraid,' Evidence said sombrely, 'that he probably lives on park benches by the sound of it.'

'Oh God,' said Gatey and burst into a fresh storm of tears.

Evidence looked round his neat, modern house, at his pretty wife bending gently over his sister and wished with all his heart that his father might not be found. He did not want him here, sitting and stinking on the three piece suite, drooling on incomprehensibly about birds or poetry or philosophy, or whatever the latest rubbish was with which he filled his addled head. He would spoil the picture. Evidence went to the sideboard and refilled his glass. He wished he hadn't had anything to do with all this nonsense from the start.

The next day was Saturday and on Monday Gatey would have to go back to London, but she decided that she would spend the weekend looking for her father. She would search every park in Manchester, every bus shelter, every nook and every darkest alley until she found him.

'You're stupid,' said Evidence. 'You'll just be wasting your time. He'll have moved on by now. These men of the road, they don't stay in one place, you know.' He shuddered involuntarily at the thought of his father being described as a 'man of the road'. 'And if you do find him – which you won't,' he added, 'don't bring him here.'

'Evidence, you're a brute,' said Gatey with feeling. 'Your own father . . .'

'Have you forgotten what he was like?' Evidence asked. 'Anyway, I don't want Milly upset.'

'Oh, come on,' said Milly, 'I see all sorts in the hospital, a tramp wouldn't bother me; in fact, I'd be quite interested in him if he was your father . . .' She broke off suddenly with a gasp and put her hand to her mouth.

'What on earth's the matter?' Evidence wanted to know.

Milly had suddenly remembered the tramp she had met in the park who had talked about poetry and daffodils in such educated tones.

'I think I may have met him,' she said simply. 'He was rather odd.'

Close cross-examination convinced Gatey beyond any reasonable doubt that the tramp in the park who had detained Milly was indeed none other than Frederick and so she became more than ever determined to spend the weekend scouring Manchester for her poor father. To Evidence's annoyance, Milly agreed to help her, but he was not really too worried as he could not imagine that they had the faintest chance of success and with Milly and Gatey out of the way he could turn his mind to other things and try to forget about his father again.

On that same Saturday morning Frederick woke up on the floor of a public lavatory somewhere in the centre of Manchester. He had spent the night there, wrapped in his old coat. When he woke he found that he was even stiffer than usual and he ached in every joint. He had been sweating and shivering in turns all night and he knew that he had a fever. His head was pounding and he was worried that if he could manage to get to his feet he might not be able to stand for long without collapsing.

'God help me, if You still exist,' he groaned. There would be no more money until next week and no more liquor unless he stole it and he knew that he had reached rock bottom. He had often felt that before, but this time it must be true. This must surely be the end of the road. The floor of a men's toilet in Manchester.

In the last few years Frederick had managed almost entirely to stifle all thoughts of the wife and children he had abandoned; memory would have been too painful, but all the same, very occasionally — at times like Christmas — their images would force themselves into his unwilling brain, causing unbearable angst. There would be Gatey's cheerful, eager face, Evidence's sulky, handsome one and, above all, Sylvia's. Where, he wondered, was she? Had she married again? Was she happy now? Then he would think that his family was far better off without him, a thought which brought a mixture of relief and added pain.

At other times he would tell himself that he was a free man and that although freedom inevitably brought with it poverty and deprivation, this was what he had chosen and it was, to a certain extent, what he had always wanted. He was perfectly aware that freedom could only be gained when you had nothing else to lose, but that, he persuaded himself, was exactly what he had bargained for.

As he lay on the floor of the men's lavatory in which

he found himself that morning, shivering and semi-delirious, Frederick imagined he saw Sylvia standing there on the grubby tiles, looking down at him with compassion. He called to her, but all at once she didn't seem to be there any longer. Things, he realised, were pretty bad, but with a febrile burst of energy he suddenly managed to stagger to his feet in the belief that he could still do something to save himself, although he was not at all clear what.

He shuffled towards the door. He must find Sylvia – she had been there only a moment ago, he had seen her – she couldn't have gone far – if he could get to the door, he'd probably find her just outside – there in the street.

'Sylvia!' he called, 'Where are you?' and he lurched through the door and collapsed onto the pavement outside.

A thickset youth in a vest, with a shaven head and a large spider tattooed on his neck, stepped over the body as it lay there, inert, blocking the way into the lavatories. But the next person who came in didn't even bother to step over Frederick, instead he kicked him in the chest and once more, idly, on the side of the head, before going on to relieve himself.

When Frederick eventually came to, his head was hurting, his chest was agony and he found breathing very painful. He was in a clean, white bed in a clean, white room and Sylvia was standing by the bed, holding his hand and smiling down at him – or was it Sylvia? A much younger Sylvia perhaps. With a mammoth effort of concentration he realised that he must be in some sort of hospital ward and this smiling angel was not Sylvia after all, but a nurse. He had no idea how he had got there, no memory of the night in the men's lavatory, no memory of passing out, of being stepped over or kicked, nor of the ambulance that had finally been called to take him to hospital.

It was a long time since Frederick had slept in a bed and despite all his discomfort, he found it strangely agreeable. What he really wanted, though, was some alcohol and he began to wonder if he would be able to get round the smiling angel at his side and persuade her to bring him some.

Gatey determinedly spent the whole weekend, sometimes on her own and sometimes in the company of Milly, searching the parks for her father. Together they traipsed all round Alexandra Park and then Chorlton Park, where Milly had originally met Frederick. Alone Gatey walked for miles along the canal and she even went to the police, but everywhere she drew a blank. She bearded a few old men of the road whom she found sleeping in doorways or on park benches, but they mostly stared at her in puzzlement and disbelief and were quite unable to help her. Only one raised a pair of bushy eyebrows and intimated that he might have seen the fellow in question a couple of weeks back. Yes, he thought he usually did stay around Manchester, but you never knew, he could have moved on. He might be anywhere by now – Cardiff, Glasgow. Gatey's heart sank as, with a quaint gesture, the old boy raised a battered hat and wished her luck.

It never occurred to Gatey to try the hospitals but, as a last resort, she called on the Samaritans. They might just have seen her father. And perhaps they had, but the kindly man who opened the door to her and even invited her in, explained that he could never reveal the identity of a caller. So there she drew another blank. By Sunday evening she was quite worn out and on Monday she left to hitch back to London, swearing that she would be back in a day or two to scour Salford.

Evidence was not at all surprised and heartily relieved by the failure of Gatey's search and he hoped that by the time she got back to London she would forget the whole thing, or at least realise that her efforts were bound to be fruitless. He hadn't slept since hearing of his father's presence in Manchester and he was beginning to feel that the whole ordered life which he had so carefully devised for himself was far more precarious than he had supposed. There was an uneasiness in the air.

He found himself beginning to be irritable with Milly and to blame her for encouraging Gatey. The whole thing was ridiculous and he even regretted the part he had played in telephoning his grandmother. By reacting to the letter she had sent to Gatey, they had only played into her hands. Gatey was wrong, Evidence felt, and even if she did succeed in tracing their father, absolutely no good could come of it.

Milly understood that Evidence felt threatened by the presence of his father in Manchester and although she sympathised with Gatey's need to find him, she half dreaded what would happen next. Perhaps Frederick had indeed moved on to Scotland or to Cornwall, that might be for the best in the end. They had done all they could – for the moment at least.

But of course Gatey could think only of her father all the way back to London and in London she suddenly became irritated by all the people lounging around in the squat, doped out of their minds; they seemed not to care about her predicament and when she told them that her father had become a tramp and that he was probably dying at that very minute in some back street in Manchester, they just giggled helplessly and pretended to be dying themselves. For once Gatey refused to join them and went angrily to bed alone. She dreamed all night about her father and woke unusually early in a state of tremendous anxiety, wondering to whom on earth she could turn for help.

When Milly went back to work after her few days off she found that she was rather relieved to be getting out of the house and away from all the tension caused by Evidence's bubbling irritation. She was glad to be away from all the fuss and bother and family drama and talk of tramps and to be able to turn her mind to something practical.

As Milly arrived, the ward sister, who was just going off duty, smiled and said, 'You should have a quiet night unless the old boy at the end on the right plays up. They brought him in two days ago – pneumonia – but his main problem seems to be the bottle. He kept the whole ward up last night shouting for a drink.'

'Perhaps he's some relation of yours, Milly,' giggled a Chinese nurse as she passed carrying a bedpan. 'He's called Appleby . . .'

Milly froze.

'Milly, are you all right?' the ward sister leaned forward urgently and took Milly by the shoulders.

'I think I'll have to sit down for a minute,' said Milly. 'We've been looking for him for the last three days.' She wondered why on earth it had never occurred to her, of all people, to ask at the hospital.

They told her that he had been brought in in a terrible condition, that he'd been found by passers-by on the pavement outside some men's toilets, kicked and bruised and half dead.

Milly wanted to cry, but the ward was short-staffed and all the beds were full and she knew that she must just pull herself together and get on with her job. At least she had all night in which to make up her mind what to do next. Certainly she had no intention of making herself known to her father-in-law until the morning and after that she would have to hand the problem over to Evidence and Gatey, although she rather doubted that either of them would have the faintest idea what to do. There was, of course, the possibility – or rather probability – that Evidence would flatly refuse to have anything whatsoever to do with his father. Milly realised that up until this moment none of them, not even she, who had seen Frederick in the park, had probably believed for a moment in his actual reappearance. It had somehow all been fantasy, even Gatey's romantic vision of a reunion with her father. What would be the reality of such a reunion, Milly wondered.

Frederick managed to remain quite quiet for most of the night. He only bellowed once. Perhaps they had given him something to make him sleep? Milly tiptoed silently up to his bed to stare intently at his sleeping face. He looked gaunter and paler and cleaner than when she had seen him last, but there was no doubt that it was the same man. She was struck by his likeness to Evidence, which of course hadn't struck her on the park bench. He must have been good-looking, she thought, before he allowed himself to get into such a mess, but now he looked a great deal older than she knew him to be, almost old enough to be her husband's grandfather – haggard, lined, grey-bearded. Evidence, she decided, would have to see him. It would be too cruel of him to refuse. But it crossed her mind that the refusal might well come from the father and not the son.

A patient called out in pain and she scuttled away down the ward to help.

At the horribly early hour when the hospital ward begins its day, temperatures are taken and cups of tea delivered, Milly approached Frederick's bed with some trepidation.

He looked at her coolly as she took the thermometer from the bracket on the wall behind the bed, frowned at it and shook it. She turned to smile at him and asked him brightly how he was feeling.

'Lousy,' he said. 'They should have left me to die on that pavement. It would have been better.'

Milly could think of nothing to say but, 'There, there,' as she put the thermometer into his mouth.

His temperature was still worryingly high despite the antibiotics that were being pumped into him.

'You'll soon be getting better now,' she said as she replaced the thermometer in its bracket, 'and then you won't feel like that.'

'Do you know,' he said, 'that before I came into this hospital – two days ago – three days ago – whenever it was, I hadn't drawn a sober breath for as long as I can remember. For three years, maybe five, ten. God only knows how long. And that is what I shall go back to.' Then he added as an afterthought, 'Do you believe in God?'

Milly didn't like that sort of question so she said, 'Why don't you drink up your tea before it gets cold?'

'Nowadays,' he said, 'nobody believes in God and no one learns any poetry at school. You can't really blame them for the first, but the second is a disgrace.'

Milly wondered if this was the moment to declare herself, to announce that she remembered meeting Frederick before and to tell him who she was, but she decided to funk it. To judge from his physical condition, he wasn't likely to be discharged for some days and she felt that she would rather go home first and confront Evidence with the truth, whether he liked it or not. She hoped Gatey would ring from London so that she could tell her what had happened, rather than having to wait for a letter to reach her.

'I'll be going off duty presently,' she said, 'but I'll see you this evening.'

'That at least will be something to look forward to,' said Frederick, without the faintest trace of suggestiveness, and he gave her a peculiarly innocent smile. 'You can tell me then whether or not you learnt any poetry at school.'

As he watched her figure retreating down the ward he felt a sudden surge of irritation, as if something were incomplete, but he had no idea what it could be. It might be something to do with what he had been saying, which seemed to find an echo somewhere in the dark recesses of his mind? But what could that echo be? Another conversation somewhere uncompleted? Something to do with the girl? How could it be? He had never seen her before. But he liked her and he liked her manner. It was a pity that they hadn't taught her any poetry at school. He began to sweat and shiver at the same time and longed to shake off his fever.

VIII

Despite the pleasantness of her manner on arriving at the station, it was not long before Lady Field settled right back into her usual habits. Sylvia wondered how on earth she would get through the ten days of her mother's visit without losing her self-control. There was no point at all in having her to stay if the whole thing was to end in a terrible quarrel which, Sylvia knew from experience, could happen only too easily. For one thing Lady Field, who loved to pass the cruellest judgments on others, could never take the slightest hint of criticism herself so that if Sylvia so much as said 'boo' a terrific conflagration would ensue.

Sylvia had of course steeled herself for her mother's arrival, but, as usual, she was amazed by the strength required to withstand the permanent assault on her self-esteem, directed at her through every imaginable channel. There were the children to be criticised, their failings attributed to their mother's weakness; there was a failed marriage to be hinted at; Frederick's hopeless drunkenness to be referred to at regular intervals; Sylvia's age, her fading hair, her fading looks, her broadening girth, her pennilessness, her position as a domestic servant, her contemptible infatuation for her dog, which could only be attributed to loneliness – all these and more were fuel for Lady Field's fire – and added to all that, just look where Sylvia was living!

'I mean, it's very drab, dear. No wonder you're depressed.' And then, 'Rather poky, isn't it?' And, 'What a pity you have to look out on that dreadful yard. I should have thought that would be enough to cast anyone down.'

'It'll be better,' said Sylvia brightly, 'when I've painted the kitchen – and maybe the sitting-room. Perhaps you would like to help me choose some paint?'

'You'll certainly need some advice about that,' said Lady Field. 'After all, interior decoration has never been your strong point. Do you remember that dreadful pink in your sitting-room when you were first married? Fuchsia or something? That's probably what made Frederick take to drink.' Lady Field shrieked with laughter at her own witticism. Sylvia gritted her teeth. They were driving into Battle to do some shopping and she thought she might take her mother to look at the Abbey and after lunch they might drive down to the coast for a walk by the sea with Prophecy. Prophecy loved the sea. By the end of all that, Sylvia hoped that her mother might be quite tired so that she would want to retire to an early bed, leaving Sylvia in peace – so long as Percy Hardcastle didn't disturb her.

Sylvia had supposed that with his daughter about Hardcastle would make fewer demands on her time and that she would just be able to do what she had to do for him and slip away quietly to her own part of the house, but this was not the case. God only knew what drama was being played out on that side of the house between father and daughter. On several occasions since Jocelyn's arrival, Sylvia had not been able to avoid overhearing Jocelyn crying, Hardcastle shouting, doors banging. Then he would suddenly burst into her kitchen, without even knocking, tears streaming down his drunken face, begging for her assistance, but unable to explain how she could help him in any way. Whenever she saw Jocelyn, she was greeted with an icy stare and a barely muttered 'good-morning' or 'good-afternoon'.

When Sylvia had taken her mother for a drink with the Hardcastles on that first evening, Jocelyn had sat moodily on the sofa without lifting her eyes from the floor and had never addressed a word to either Sylvia or Lady Field. She had only spoken in the curtest possible way to her father, who had burbled on incomprehensibly about apparently nothing. Sylvia had made her getaway as soon as she decently could with Lady Field following indignantly behind her.

'Well, I must say,' Lady Field declared before they were truly out of earshot, 'there must be something about you my dear, that makes you choose those kind of men. Out of the frying-pan into the fire. I would have thought that you might have learnt something from your experiences with Frederick. The only difference, as far as I can see, is that at least this man's got some money.'

Sylvia couldn't let that pass. How dared her mother compare Percy Hardcastle to Frederick – and besides, her relationship to Hardcastle was purely a business one.

'We shall see,' said Lady Field with a knowing nod.

So it was just as Sylvia had feared: between her mother and Hardcastle there was no time for Wilf, whose comforting presence she missed so dreadfully. She longed for him to be there so that she could tell him what was happening and to share with him the monstrosity of her life. Wilf, she felt sure, was a most understanding man, but still she was surprised by the strength of her feeling for him. She wondered if he would call at all while her mother was staying and rather feared that he might not, out of some misplaced sense of tact. But despite her longing to see him, she couldn't help hoping in one tiny corner of her heart that he would stay away as she dreaded the embarrassment her mother would cause her in front of him, talking down to him and playing the Lady.

She thought that perhaps he would call one evening after Lady Field had retired to bed, but then, as likely as not, he would find Hardcastle weeping in her kitchen. She played with the idea of purposefully breaking a sash-cord, or taking the washer out of a tap so as to have an excuse to call for him, but, if she did that, he would be sure to come at an hour when Lady Field was in full battle cry and she wouldn't have a chance to talk to him.

In the evening after the walk by the sea, Lady Field did indeed decide to go early to bed and having declared herself to be utterly exhausted she went upstairs at a quarter to nine.

'Most unlike me not to sit up for the ten o'clock news headlines,' she announced as she left the room. 'But you have quite worn me out, my dear. It's been a long day for your mother.'

As the door closed behind Lady Field, Sylvia sighed gently and tousled Prophecy's head. 'What shall we do now?' she asked the dog, who looked longingly up at her mistress with sorrowful eyes and wagged an indolent tail. Sylvia sat there for a moment with the dog before deciding to make herself a cup of coffee and she had just turned on the kettle when she heard a knock at the outside door. She caught her breath and hurried to see who was there. As usual it was raining outside. When she opened the door she was sure that her delight at seeing Wilf must have shown all over her face, but it didn't matter.

'Come on in out of the wet,' she said as Wilf hesitated to cross the threshold. 'My mother's gone to bed. There's no one here and I was just about to make some coffee. Would you like some?'

'I hoped you wouldn't mind my calling,' said Wilf, 'but I was passing and I just wondered if you were all right, what with one thing and another?' He nodded at the ceiling and then at the wall dividing Sylvia's kitchen from the front of the house.

Sylvia could have flung her arms around his neck. She felt that she had never, ever been so pleased to see anyone in her life.

'Oh, I'm just so glad you've come! Sit down,' she said, 'I'm dying to tell you everything that's been going on.' She looked at Wilf and smiled. He smiled back at her and she thought what nice grey eyes he had in his pale, lined face and wondered if he was as pleased to see her as she was to see him. She hoped so.

One of these days, she thought, I'll surprise everybody and I'll run away with Wilf Wapshott and live in his cottage at the end of the village and cook his tea and iron his shirts and sleep in his bed and together we'll take Prophecy for walks on Sunday afternoons. Suddenly she felt herself blush at her own thoughts and at the innocence of the idyll she imagined for herself.

'Well,' she said briskly, 'all sorts of things have been going on next door since I last saw you and my mother has been doing her best to drive me mad . . .' She broke off what she was saying, astounded by a terrific noise of banging and shouting that was coming from next door. 'It's been going on like that all the time,' she said.

'It's terrible and quite embarrassing. I can't help over-hearing them. And they hardly stop when I'm in there cooking their supper.'

'How long's Jocelyn staying?' Wilf wanted to know.

'I've no idea,' said Sylvia, 'but I can't imagine she'd want to stay for long with all that going on. Perhaps she's trying to stop him from drinking, but I could tell her not to waste her time.' Then she added sadly, 'My husband used to drink. I probably told you.' But she still didn't tell him that she had been married to a clergyman.

Sylvia and Wilf were sitting at her kitchen table, drinking whisky and talking an hour later, and Wilf may even have had his hand over Sylvia's when the connecting door burst open without warning and Percy Hardcastle staggered in. He had a glass in his hand and the inevitable bleary, unfocused look in his eyes. He stopped dead when he saw Wilf.

'What the hell are you doing here?' he blurted out.

Wilf didn't deign to answer, but merely said, 'Good-evening Mr Hardcastle.'

Sylvia simply stared in amazement at Hardcastle, thunderstruck by his ill manners and totally at a loss for anything to say, which she realised as she sat there in silence was just as well, for she had learnt the hard way that it was a complete waste of time to speak to anyone in such a drunken state. She merely wished that she could remember to keep the intercommunicating door locked if her privacy was to be invaded in this way.

'I won't have people sitting around in my house after closing hours!' Hardcastle roared inconsequently, then stumbled as he lurched angrily towards the table where Wilf was sitting. 'You'd better be going,' he said as he steadied himself on the back of the chair.

Wilf didn't move.

'I think you're the one who had better be going,' he said quietly. 'Why don't you go home and sleep it off . . .'

Sylvia's heart stopped as Hardcastle took another lurch forward towards Wilf. She had seen the look in Hardcastle's eye and was sure that he was going to hit him. And he probably was, but instead, he tripped and fell headlong to the floor and passed out.

Wilf smiled wryly and said 'Poor bugger. We'll have to try to get him back next door somehow.'

Sylvia looked at the huge man on the floor and despaired, she could see him there still in the morning and hear her mother's insistent tones, continuously comparing Hardcastle to Frederick and harping on about his money.

'We'd better prop the door open,' said Wilf getting up. 'You take one arm and I'll take the other and we'll drag him . . . put him on a sofa somewhere because I don't think we'll get him upstairs. Better lay him on his side, he might vomit and choke.'

Sylvia did as she was told, thinking the while that she had certainly been there before. Poor Frederick, she suddenly thought. How undignified to have descended to this.

They were dragging the stupefied body through the hall to Hardcastle's sitting-room when they suddenly heard footsteps. They both looked up simultaneously to see Jocelyn standing on the stairs, looking down at them, ice-cold as Cruella Deville. Somehow in the commotion Sylvia had completely forgotten about Jocelyn.

'It's your father,' she said foolishly.

'That's quite obvious,' said Cruella. 'Put him in the sitting-room and get out – both of you.'

Wilf was a strong man but it was a struggle, even

with Sylvia's help, to get Hardcastle up on the sofa, but they somehow managed. All the time Sylvia was horribly aware of Jocelyn's cold presence on the stairs outside in the hall. They tiptoed out of the sitting-room and closed the door gently and as they crossed the hall Sylvia turned and said to Jocelyn, 'Perhaps it would be a good idea to put a blanket over him.'

'One day he'll die alone here by choking on his own vomit,' was all the reply she made.

Sylvia and Wilf scuttled like mice confronted by a huge tom-cat back to Sylvia's kitchen, where they closed the intercommunicating door and locked it firmly.

'Then she'll get the money,' said Wilf. 'I reckon that's all she's waiting for.'

Not so very long ago Sylvia had been very depressed, dragging herself from dreary task to dreary task and returning to her kitchen, as often as not to sink wearily down to the floor to put her arms around her beloved dog. Then she had supposed that she had no option but to stick it out with Percy Hardcastle, thankful at least that she had a roof over her head. Now she suddenly realised for the first time that it was a little while since she had felt that way. In fact, Wilf had brought light back into her life and with the light came renewed vigour, optimism and, she supposed, an ability to take charge of events.

She wondered now if she really could stick the horrors of the Hardcastle household indefinitely, or whether she would have to move on. But she knew that she could not move if it meant losing Wilf. He, she knew, would miss her dreadfully too and she, she imagined, would simply revert to lying on the floor beside Prophecy because in fact nothing else had changed except the appearance of Wilf as a confidant and friend.

'You shouldn't be here alone with that man,' Wilf remarked as they settled down to yet another cup of coffee. 'It's no good.'

'I'm all right,' said Sylvia. 'Well, I will be as long as I keep that door locked.'

'But if he came banging on the door and it was locked you'd just go and open it,' Wilf said.

Sylvia knew that that was a problem that she would have to deal with when the occasion arose, but she had settled into her new home now; she felt all right where she was in a funny way.

'In fact,' she said, 'I haven't been so happy for a long time.'

Wilf gave her a sidelong glance and said that he ought to be going. He kissed her good-night at the door and she squeezed his hand and said thank you and felt even happier than before.

'I'll be round in the morning,' he said, 'just to make sure you're all right, but if I were you I'd be looking for somewhere else to go. There are plenty of single men around looking for housekeepers.'

Sylvia thought of her earlier fantasy about Wilf's cottage and wondered exactly what he meant by that remark. Exactly what he said, she supposed.

'Good-night,' she said and closed the door behind him as he stepped out into the interminable rain.

Wilf was round again in the morning quite early. Lady Field, who had been sitting having her breakfast, let him in as Sylvia was next door making the Hardcastles theirs.

Hardcastle appeared, bleary-eyed and crumpled from his night on the sofa. He clearly had no recollection of the events that had led up to it.

'What on earth's the time?' he asked. 'I thought it was the middle of the night. Funny, I must have fallen asleep on the sofa.'

'Are you ready for your breakfast?' Sylvia wanted to know. He looked as if he was ready for the grave.

'Where's Jocelyn?' was all he said.

'I suppose she's still asleep,' Sylvia said. Jocelyn didn't usually appear until well past midday.

'Leave all that now,' Hardcastle said. 'I don't want any breakfast this morning. I'll see you later.' He paused and then said quite kindly, 'Sylvia, I don't know what I'd do without you.'

Back in her own kitchen Sylvia found Wilf standing awkwardly just inside the outside door, with his cap in his hand, while her mother sat pontificating at the kitchen table.

'I was just telling this young man,' she said, 'that he'll have to wait until I've finished my breakfast to do whatever it is that he's come to do. I can't have workmen around while I'm eating. That, of course, is the trouble with this modern habit of not having a dining-room. Sir Kenneth Field and I always used to take our breakfast in the dining-room. So much more civilised . . .'

'Good-morning, Wilf,' Sylvia interrupted the flow.

'Hallo, Sylvia, how are things with you this morning?' Wilf asked.

Lady Field said nothing, she merely sniffed, closed her eyes and raised her eyebrows. Enormous disapproval emanated from her person.

'By the way, this is my mother,' Sylvia said, 'and Mummy, this is Wilf Wapshott, he's a friend of mine.' Sylvia felt wonderfully defiant as the disapproval emanating from Lady Field thickened. 'Well, Wilf,' she went on, 'perhaps we should let my mother have her breakfast in peace, so let's go into the sitting-room.'

'I don't suppose it occurs to you that you ought to be looking after your mother?' Lady Field said with barely controlled anger. 'After all, I didn't expect to come all the way here just to be ignored.' As Wilf and Sylvia left the room she began to mutter to herself in a loud stage whisper, 'I sometimes wonder where she was brought up – and what's this tea she buys, I'd like to know? Some cheap muck I suppose. She might have got something a bit better for her mother.'

'If that was anyone other than your mother,' Wilf said when they reached the sitting-room, 'I'd be tempted to call her a proper bitch.'

'I'm afraid that's just what she is,' Sylvia said smiling, 'but she's old and she's lonely and I feel sorry for her.'

'It seems to me that you're frightened of her,' Wilf suggested. 'Anyway, how's the old boy this morning? Seen him?'

Sylvia told Wilf what had happened with Hardcastle and that she hadn't seen Jocelyn at all since last night.

'I'll probably see her some time today,' she said, 'but it won't be very pleasant. I can't say I'm looking forward to that.' Then she felt that after the forced intimacy and unusual circumstances of the night before she could ask Wilf to call again that evening after her mother had gone to bed. 'But come a little later,' she said, 'she doesn't usually go to bed until after the ten o'clock news headlines.'

Wilf pretended that it would be no more than his duty to come round in the evening, just to make sure that Hardcastle wasn't creating and that Jocelyn hadn't given Sylvia too hard a time.

She thanked him from the bottom of her heart and hoped with every fibre of her being that it wasn't just to protect her from Hardcastle that he wanted to come. 'I'd better go back and look after my mother now,' she said. 'Thank you for coming.'

As Wilf walked through the kitchen to leave the house Lady Field snorted very loudly.

Sylvia felt that the certainty of Wilf's arrival in the evening would make it possible for her to weather whatever storm, or storms, lay in wait for her that day.

The comforting thought had barely crossed her mind when Lady Field remarked tartly, 'Cocky little man that. I wouldn't trust him if I were you, he doesn't seem to know his place.'

Sylvia pretended not to have heard. She had to go back next door to do a few jobs, the prospect of which made her feel rather uneasy, she particularly did not relish the thought of a confrontation with Jocelyn, but perhaps Jocelyn was still in bed.

Jocelyn was indeed still in bed, but her father was sitting brooding over a cup of strong tea when Sylvia reappeared in his kitchen.

'Sit down,' he said in a maudlin voice and he patted the table beside him. 'I want to talk to you.'

Sylvia's heart sank. 'I've got one or two jobs I must do – the laundry,' she said brightly.

'Never mind that, it can all wait,' said Hardcastle, patting the table more insistently. 'Do sit down, please.' There was an urgency in his manner.

'So what is the problem?' Sylvia sat down stiffly. She was determined to keep her distance.

'I am a very unhappy man,' Hardcastle replied.

Sylvia felt like retorting sharply that if he laid off the drink that might help, but instead she murmured, 'Oh dear,' sympathetically.

'And Sylvia . . .'

She had inadvertently left her hand on the table but

tried to pull it away smartly as his heavy hand advanced to cover it. His hand fell with a pathetic thump on the table.

'I have fallen in love with a very beautiful woman . . .'

'Who is she?' Sylvia asked and then blushed as she had never blushed before. How could she be so stupid and how could he be so cumbersome?

Hardcastle gazed balefully at her. 'Don't you know who she is?' he asked. Suddenly he threw his shoulders back and appeared to take some sort of a grip on himself.

'I,' he said with all the pomposity he could muster, 'am a very wealthy man and I would like you to be my wife.'

'No, Mr Hardcastle – Percy,' she forced the word 'Percy' through her lips – 'No, I'm afraid that that won't do.' What wouldn't do, she wondered. The man? The offer? The way it was put? Everything. What was she to do? She could hardly stay as Hardcastle's house-keeper once she had turned down his offer of marriage, but if she left, where would she go? Above all, how would she see Wilf? The only other suitable job she might find could well be in Harrogate – or Truro – a long way away from Wilf.

She was standing up suddenly. 'Oh God,' she said, 'what a muddle!'

Hardcastle couldn't see what the fuss was about and had clearly not expected anything other than immediate acceptance. 'There is no muddle,' he said, 'I, as I have said, am a very wealthy man and I am in need of a wife. You are not a wealthy woman and you are clearly in need of a husband. I had long dreamed that my daugh-ter, Jocelyn, whom I love, would come and keep me company here, but this, I'm afraid, seems increasingly unlikely. Besides, Sylvia,' he re-adopted the baleful look, 'I have grown increasingly fond of you.'

'I'm sorry,' said Sylvia. 'It is impossible, quite out of the question, but,' she added as an afterthought, 'I am very touched.'

Hardcastle suddenly jumped to his feet and caught at Sylvia's arm which he held in an almost painful grip. 'Don't say that,' he begged. 'Just don't say that. You can have no idea of the unhappiness I have been going through – of the bogies which come to haunt me in the night. You cannot leave me – you wouldn't . . .'

'Mr Hardcastle,' said Sylvia, regaining her poise, 'let us try to forget that this conversation has ever taken place.' He must have already forgotten so many conversations he had had before in his cups – why not this one? 'Let's just forget it and try to continue as normal. I must check the laundry now.'

Under an apparently calm exterior Sylvia felt completely overwhelmed. There was Hardcastle, passing out in her kitchen one evening and proposing to her the next morning and there was Wilf, whom she loved, being insulted by her mother and there was her mother sitting like an old crow emanating poison in her kitchen. She left the room slowly, in what she hoped was a dignified manner.

'I'll come and see you this evening,' Hardcastle said to her back, 'after your mother's gone to bed.'

Lady Field finished her breakfast and slowly began to clear her things away, but she had no idea where anything belonged so she left her cup and saucer and plate dripping on the draining board. In fact, her poor eyesight had prevented her from washing them properly so that crumbs stuck to the plate and lipstick to the cup. Nevertheless the whole process took her some time, during which she considered what her next line of attack would be. Sylvia was quite obviously in a silly frame of mind – due to her age her mother presumed – but it really would not do for her to be consorting with odd job men. What would Sir Kenneth have thought? Besides, the man was a thoroughly shifty-looking character. How naïve of Sylvia to be taken in by someone so transparent. But then of course Sylvia had always been naïve. And what had he been doing coming to call at such an early hour? What indeed? It didn't seem to Lady Field that he had really come to mend something. No, she didn't trust the man.

What Sylvia really ought to do was to marry the man next door. Plenty of money there and when you came to think about it, he wasn't such a bad man after all; Sylvia certainly had no right to expect anything better. In fact, she would be very lucky indeed to catch him.

As Sylvia came back into the kitchen Lady Field decided that the time was right to have a word with her daughter. She was sitting there knitting a pink bedjacket.

'I should think that Percy Hardcastle is a very shrewd man,' she began. 'I'm not a complete fool, you know, and I have learned a thing or two in life. You could do a lot worse.'

Sylvia said nothing.

'Quite a nice-looking man,' Lady Field commented stubbornly.

Sylvia looked at her mother as if she were mad. 'What?' she said.

'Quite a nice-looking man,' Lady Field repeated, 'and generous, too, I should imagine.' Her knitting-needles clicked ominously.

'What about the fact that he drinks too much?' Sylvia asked.

'Oh darling, you should be able to cope with that –

well, I should have thought that you'd have had quite enough experience of that not to let it bother you.'

'Yes, quite enough.'

'Perhaps he'd had a little too much the other night, but I expect he was celebrating the arrival of his daughter – after all, you tell me that she hasn't been to see him for some time. Even you can't expect a man not to have a drop too much once in a while. In my opinion, Percy Hardcastle is a real man – and a gentleman.' In a momentary flash of enlightenment it dawned on Lady Field that what she was saying was not finding total favour with her daughter, so she decided to change her tack.

'I wouldn't wonder,' she said darkly, 'if every single, middle-aged woman within miles didn't have her eye on him. I should think he's got the pick of the county.' She relapsed into her former mode, 'I mean, at your age you can't expect Gary Glitter.'

'Gary Glitter?' Sylvia said forlornly.

'Well, you know what I mean – you can't pick and choose and you have to face facts: there you are, the divorced, penniless wife of a drunken parson – and not exactly Joan Collins – what are you waiting for?' Lady Field wondered whether or not to say any more about the drunken parson and his possible whereabouts at this juncture, but she decided against it for the time being; she wanted to keep some cards up her sleeve.

Sylvia was wondering why on earth she ever bothered to have anything to do with this woman – what made her feel any obligation to her at all? She felt like screaming, but she knew that it would serve no purpose. There was no point, either, in arguing about Gary Glitter or Percy Hardcastle or any other nonsense. There was no point in saying that she, Sylvia, was not fat, or old, or plain, or stupid, because that was precisely what her mother would have liked her to do. Lady Field wanted her daughter to mind all the nasty things she was saying and, in her present mood, she also wanted her to marry Hardcastle because that would bring money and, in her opinion, standing and would also keep Sylvia in a vulnerable position. If Sylvia were to find a man of her own choosing and be happy, Lady Field would be mortified. So Sylvia said nothing. But she also said nothing because she was afraid of her mother, and she knew this to be the case. She wondered if she would ever be able to truly not mind what her mother said – perhaps even be able to turn to her and say so. Of course now, when she was at last beginning to think that she might be able to summon up the courage, it was becoming increasingly difficult because her mother was getting old and you couldn't really be unkind or impatient with an old lady.

'So what are we going to do today – or will you be too busy to have time to bother about your old mother?' Lady Field suddenly wanted to know.

Sylvia thought of Wilf and the knowledge that she would be seeing him that evening made her feel quite calm. She had a few jobs to do, but there was no reason why she shouldn't take her mother for an outing after lunch.

'What would you like to do, Mummy? After all, it's your holiday,' Sylvia said sweetly. For a moment she had forgotten that Hardcastle had threatened to disrupt her evening.

IX

When Jocelyn woke and reached out one long, thin, white arm for her watch from the bedside table she felt it was late. It was after half-past twelve. She swore mildly out loud and stretched. She supposed she ought to be getting up, but she dreaded the thought of the day ahead and wondered if her father had already started drinking. Then she remembered the scene last night, when she had found those two from next door dragging her stupefied father across the hall. She had felt very angry with both them and him, in fact, she had felt so angry that she had merely turned on her heels and gone to bed as soon as Sylvia and Wilf had gone, without bothering to go and see how her father was. She certainly hadn't taken a blanket to him. Why should she trouble herself over him when he was so unwilling to pay her bills for her? Ever since she had got home there had been these endless rows about money. Of course Hardcastle would pay in the end, he would have to and he knew that as well as she did. The alternative could be too unpleasant for him and his hand was forced.

Perhaps the woman next door had something to do with it all; it didn't seem to Jocelyn that her father had ever been so difficult about money before. He had usually dished it out quite easily. Perhaps he had been hoping for something in return? Well, as far as Jocelyn was concerned, he had had all he was ever going to get out of her. She supposed that he had ruined her life and she hated him for that and yet the power which she sensed she had over him gave her a kind of buzz that in some peculiar way tied her to him, even attracted her to him.

Jocelyn was suspicious of Sylvia and had a kind of feeling in her bones that Sylvia was after her father's money. After all, it couldn't be much fun acting as a housekeeper to a maudlin alcoholic and if Sylvia was prepared to stay and do the job, wouldn't she be better off as his wife? It would obviously be enormously to her advantage. It was strange what some people would do for money. Besides, it was quite clear that Hardcastle had taken a great liking to Sylvia, which was something that had never happened before with any of his earlier housekeepers, all of whom he had treated with tremendous arrogance. Jocelyn had to admit that she could see why her father liked Sylvia, who was undoubtedly a pretty woman – a little faded and rather sad looking – but definitely pretty, with remarkable eyes and the sort of gentle manner that a maudlin old fool like her father would obviously go for. There was a quiet certainty, too, about Sylvia, which made Jocelyn realise that she would be no mean adversary.

She stretched again and slowly pushed back the bedclothes. She rolled lazily out of bed and stood for a moment, naked, in front of the long mirror to admire herself. She thought she was very beautiful indeed as she pushed up her chin and ran her fingers through her hair. Perhaps she should go for the rich lord after all.

As she pulled on a pair of black velveteen, skin-tight jodhpurs, she wondered how best to conduct her offensive against Sylvia. She was determined that that woman would not get her hands on her father's money, which for every possible reason was hers by right. Suddenly it occurred to her that Sylvia herself had played into her hands. What had that fellow, Wilf Wapshott, been doing with Sylvia last night? Nothing, probably, and as Sylvia's ghastly mother was next door too, Wilf's presence could hardly have been very significant. But that didn't matter, the whole thing was quite convenient and Jocelyn was determined to put it to the best possible use. She'd see Sylvia out of the house before she went back to London. And her mother, too.

Downstairs in the kitchen Hardcastle was contemplating the hair of the dog that bit him. He felt bloody awful, so awful in fact that he could hardly face getting up to go and help himself to a drink, but he needed one. All this hoo-ha about Jocelyn's bills was too much for him and on top of that there was Sylvia's irrational rejection of him. He missed his daughter dreadfully when she wasn't there, but when she did come home it always seemed to cause such an upheaval and then he would look at her and feel proud and guilty and desirous all at once. No wonder a man needed an occasional drink. He didn't really think he drank too much – certainly not on a regular basis, but he needed one this morning to help him to think about Sylvia and before he could face Jocelyn's haughty anger again, and he could hear her moving about upstairs now. Beautiful Jocelyn, who had tempted him so and who was surely just as much to blame as he.

The smell of the lasagne Sylvia had left cooking in the Aga was making Hardcastle feel sick. He decided, with a mammoth effort, to go and fetch a gin and tonic – just to settle the stomach.

Jocelyn came slowly downstairs just as her father was returning to the kitchen with a brimming glass.

'How many of those have you already had this morning?' she asked coolly.

Hardcastle's hand was so unsteady that he had to take a huge gulp from his drink for fear of spilling it before he sat down.

'I've been sitting here reading the paper all morning,' he said, 'just waiting for you to get up.'

Jocelyn went across to the Aga and opened the door to see what was cooking.

'Pff . . .' she said, screwing up her nose, 'what's this muck?'

'Lasagne,' said Hardcastle. 'Sylvia is a very good cook, it's for our lunch and I don't doubt that it is excellent.' In fact as Jocelyn opened the oven door, the pungent smell made his stomach lurch so that he wondered if he would be able to face eating any of it at all.

Jocelyn began to make herself some coffee. 'I don't like lasagne,' she said.

'It hasn't got any meat in it if that's what you think,' said Hardcastle. He wished they didn't have to go on talking about that food.

'You can have it if you want,' said Jocelyn, 'but I'm not eating any of it.' She sat down at the table opposite her father with a mug of black coffee, which she stirred idly.

'You must be feeling pretty rotten this morning,' she said and stared at him long and hard.

He avoided her gaze. 'I don't know why you should think that,' he said.

'Do you know what happened last night?' she asked brutally.

'Nothing much,' said Hardcastle, and he drained his gin and tonic and began to get unsteadily to his feet.

Jocelyn looked at him with a mixture of disgust and pity. He was so steeped in alcohol nowadays that a couple of drinks were enough to send him over the top and he would be drunk again in a moment.

'Just don't get another drink yet, for God's sake,' she almost pleaded.

Unaccountably, Hardcastle slumped back onto his chair.

'You know,' he said, 'it's only since you've been here that I've been drinking. You must believe me. It's all the tension and the worry about you and your money problems.' He buried his head in his hands in despair and wished as he spoke that he hadn't mentioned money.

'It's just as well you don't remember what happened last night if you ask me,' Jocelyn said. 'I won't tell you as it would only distress you.' She smiled sweetly at her father as she spoke and blew him a kiss across the table.

Hardcastle felt the prickly sweat of fear break out on the back of his neck. Oh Christ, what had he done now?

'Isn't it lucky,' Jocelyn spoke so quietly that she almost whispered, 'that the parishioners — the people you preach to on Sundays in that church out there,' she extended an elegant arm and pointed out of the window, 'isn't it lucky that they don't know what goes on in here behind the scenes?' She laughed a merry laugh.

Hardcastle couldn't take any more. He staggered to his feet and left the kitchen to fill his glass from the decanter in the sitting-room.

But Jocelyn hadn't finished with him. She stood up and followed him slowly to the other room.

Hardcastle was racking his brain to remember the events of the night before. He remembered having supper with his daughter – he thought he could even remember what they had eaten, so he couldn't have been that drunk. He couldn't remember anything else. Well, nothing much else could have happened – no, nothing could have happened – not any longer – he was sure of it. He'd woken up this morning on the sofa, that was true, but he'd probably just fallen asleep watching television. There was nothing wrong with that. He poured himself a drink.

Jocelyn stood behind him with her coffee cup in her hand. 'You ought to be careful you know, people might start talking . . .'

'What the hell are you going on about? You know nothing happened at all last night, you're just trying to frighten me.' Hardcastle had swung round to face his daughter.

'And they all came in here from next door because of the shindy,' said Jocelyn. 'God only knows what they must have thought.'

'Who came in from next door?' Hardcastle bellowed. He didn't want Sylvia dragged into these awful rows. He liked Sylvia, respected her; he was thinking of marrying her. She was a good woman.

'Who do you think? That Sylvia, of course, and her boyfriend.'

Hardcastle had no idea what Jocelyn was going on about. He had no memory of Sylvia coming to see them the evening before, and what on earth did Jocelyn mean by talking about a boyfriend? 'You talk nonsense,' he said, 'Sylvia hasn't got a boyfriend. There hasn't been a man here to see her since she came.'

'That's what you think, Dad,' said Jocelyn calmly, 'but what about that little builder fellow – Alf – Wilf – whatever he's called?'

Hardcastle was astounded. He'd never heard so much nonsense.

'Wapshott!' he said. 'Little Wilf Wapshott? He's nobody's boyfriend, he's the odd job man.'

Jocelyn laughed again. 'You are an innocent, Dad,' she said, and left the room.

Hardcastle scratched his head and frowned. What the hell was going on? Jocelyn was just telling stories to confuse him. He staggered towards the sofa and sank down into it. He kept on frowning and scratching his head. Something was bothering him but he couldn't think what it was. Could it be something to do with Wilf Wapshott? Had he seen him somewhere recently? Had he perhaps said something to the man? He couldn't think of anything, but he knew that until he had solved the problem, little Wilf Wapshott would remain fixed irritatingly, like a line of half-remembered poetry, in the corner of his mind.

There was no doubt about it that Jocelyn's opening offensive had had an effect and she was very pleased with herself. So pleased in fact that she even consented to sit and eat some lasagne with her father, who miraculously managed to remain more or less sober throughout lunch and even to mess with a little lasagne on his plate. She wondered if she had shocked him into sobriety, but then that would have been no bad thing. Now she could at last envisage herself going back to London within a day or two armed with a fat cheque; she couldn't wait to go.

After lunch Jocelyn took herself out for a walk because she couldn't bear the atmosphere in the house any longer. She couldn't bear the sight of her alternately angry and cringing father and neither could she bear the horrible, haunting memories of the past, which his presence – or her presence at home – inevitably aroused. Sometimes she thought that she had been turned by it all into a very nasty person, but more usually she saw herself as someone who had been made, through no fault of her own, to suffer grotesquely and who was obliged to fight forever for her corner. If she didn't fight for her own survival what grain of self-respect would be left to her? In her behaviour towards her father there was no room for pity, compassion, or forgiveness and yet her feelings towards him were unbelievably complicated. It would be best, of course, if she were never to see him. He didn't deserve her – this beautiful daughter whose trust he had betrayed. If only her mother had lived, things would surely have been different. Jocelyn tried not to think of her mother because when she did she was often overwhelmed by a violent, impotent rage directed at her for having died when she did.

Hardcastle felt quite relieved when his daughter announced her intention of going out for a while. He, too, was worn out with all the emotion and he had a sermon to attend to, but as he was feeling so tired he decided to see first of all if there was an afternoon film on the television and within a few minutes he was sound asleep and snoring on the sofa with his head back, hands folded over his ample belly and his legs stretched out in front of him.

He woke with a start a couple of hours later and was surprised to find how long he had been asleep. He wondered if Jocelyn had come back yet; if she had, she might well have just retired to her room. He didn't feel up to any further confrontation at the moment, so he

136

hoped she wouldn't reappear at least until he had made himself a cup of tea.

As he waited for the kettle to boil he began to think about Sylvia again. He had said that he loved her, and this he believed to be true; she would certainly make him an ideal wife and, as he had pointed out to her, he was a very wealthy man. He couldn't see any obstacle to a happy solution. Perhaps Sylvia had been taken too much by surprise and if he gave her a little time to think, everything would fall into place nicely.

Then he remembered Wilf Wapshott. What was all this rubbish about Wapshott and why did it bother him so? Of course Sylvia couldn't prefer a man like that to himself – an uneducated man with no money! It was ridiculous to suppose that she would rather live in a humble little working man's cottage than in a nice house like this. Jocelyn could be quite a troublemaker; of course she had invented the whole thing – and yet – and yet – something troubled him. It was a nuisance about that Lady Field woman being there, if she weren't, he could have gone to see Sylvia to get a straight answer from her. He had told her he would go through and see her later that evening and that, he thought, would be the best thing to do, but he felt impatient. For the moment he would retire to his study and think about his sermon.

Sylvia was sitting with her mother in the sitting-room watching the television, not that Sylvia was paying any attention whatsoever to a documentary about the homeless, she was daydreaming about Wilf and thinking how extraordinary it was and how quite unexpected that she should suddenly have fallen in love again at her age. And why with Wilf? It might be, she knew, just because she was lonely and he was there, but she hated to think that that was the reason. She hated to think that under the circumstances she could have fallen for anyone who happened to present themselves. That would be unworthy, somehow, and an insult to Wilf. After all, she would never in a million years have fallen for Percy Hardcastle. And what on earth was she to do about him, she wondered? Her life had suddenly become very complicated.

But about Wilf there was something exceptional, of that Sylvia was sure . . . and in her mind she enumerated what she saw as his endless qualities of kindness, humour, honesty and so forth. Fate, she decided, had brought them together at a time when each was in need of the other. Then she began to torture herself about what Wilf must be thinking of her. He might well not see the relationship developing along the same lines that she did. She blushed at the thought of the humiliation that might lie ahead. Wilf had made it quite clear that he was fond of Sylvia and that he valued her companionship, but, for all she knew, his fondness for her went just so far and no further. She sighed and wished she was ten years younger. It must be ridiculous of her at her age to entertain such hopes of romance . . .

Lady Field was knitting and snorting as she watched the television.

'If some of these people did a job and stopped relying on the Government for everything, they might not be homeless,' she said.

'It doesn't look as if the Government has given them very much,' said Sylvia, abandoning her reverie for a moment.

'In my opinion,' said Lady Field, 'they should be kept off the streets. They're an insult to decent people and a disgrace to the country. What on earth must foreigners think when they come here?'

Sylvia forbore to argue with her mother. There would have been no point.

'I've seen people like them,' said Lady Field, 'in Manchester.' She paused for effect but Sylvia was thinking about Wilf again and counting the time till his arrival.

'In the Arndale Centre,' Lady Field went on. 'Right there in the city centre.' She sensed that Sylvia was not really listening. She knew how to make her listen, though. 'I was there only the other day,' she said, 'and there was this tramp – this perfectly filthy tramp – long, grey beard – nits in his head – string keeping his trousers up,' Lady Field was warming to her theme, 'fly buttons undone, I shouldn't wonder,' she said, 'and drunk as a lord, of course . . .'

Suddenly the telephone rang, interrupting Lady Field just as she was about to reach her thrilling *dénouement*. She clicked her teeth and knitted furiously as Sylvia got up to answer the telephone.

Sylvia was surprised to hear Jocelyn's voice at the end of the line, sounding unusually polite and even friendly.

'I'm so sorry to bother you,' said Jocelyn sweetly, 'but I wondered if I could possibly come through and have a quick word with you for a moment.'

Sylvia was amazed. What on earth could Jocelyn want to say to her? But she was beguiled by the charming, appealing manner. 'Of course,' she said, 'do come. My mother and I were only just sitting here watching the television. I'll come and open the door for you.' She suddenly felt embarrassed at having to admit that the interconnecting door was locked, but thought that if Jocelyn had an ounce of intelligence she would know exactly why it was.

Lady Field was most annoyed at having been interrupted just as she was about to reveal all and properly capture her daughter's attention.

'I don't really know why I bother to come and see you,' she said. 'No one ever listens to what I have to say – and if you did listen, you might even find that your old mother wasn't quite so much of a fool as you like to think.'

'I'm so sorry,' said Sylvia with feeling, 'of course no one thinks you're a fool, it's just the telephone, I had to answer it. It was Jocelyn – I can't think what she wants, but I must just go and let her in.'

'Knit one, slip one, knit two, pass slip stitch over,' Lady Field muttered angrily, furiously scowling at her knitting, with her back half-turned to her daughter. 'Very rude young woman,' she said aloud to herself as Sylvia left the room. 'She needs to learn some manners before she's allowed in here, if you ask me.'

Sylvia came back with Jocelyn, who was smiling angelically.

'Do sit down,' she said, addressing Jocelyn, despite herself, as if she were a really important person. 'Would you like some coffee?'

'Black, please, with no sugar,' Jocelyn replied as she sat down and then, leaning towards Lady Field she remarked brightly, 'What lovely wool! What are you knitting?'

Jocelyn had worked her plan of campaign out quite carefully. The lunch time offensive against her father had had an effect, but so as to be sure of success she would also have to deal with Sylvia. Without her interference Sylvia could simply deny that she had anything to do with the odd job man and Hardcastle would certainly believe her, and then they would be back to square one and before Jocelyn could bat an eyelid, Sylvia and he would be married and she would be out in the cold without a penny to her name.

When Sylvia came back with the coffee Jocelyn smiled sweetly again and said, 'I was just admiring Lady Field's knitting. Isn't it lovely? I wish I could do something like that, but I'm afraid I'd never have the patience.'

Sylvia looked at her steadily and wondered what on earth she could be getting at.

'It must be nice to come back to the country and get out of London sometimes,' she said, by way of polite conversation. 'And of course your father must be thrilled.'

'I only wish I could manage to get away more often,' Jocelyn cooed and drawled all at once, 'because I simply adore it here – and, of course, poor Dad, he's so dreadfully lonely, I mean, it must be awful for him since Mum died and all that . . .' Jocelyn looked at the floor and allowed her voice to trail away.

Sylvia felt more and more uneasy.

'You see, it's all been so fantastically difficult since Mum . . .' Jocelyn glanced at Lady Field and then at Sylvia and back at Lady Field. She was glad the old bag was there too. She looked again at Sylvia with a long, cool, hard stare and ran a hand through her dark curls. 'I mean,' she hunched up her shoulders and hummed and hawed, 'it was obviously awful for Dad, having a teenage daughter to bring up – and I was impossible – quite impossible – I really can't imagine how he coped. And now I'm in London, so for the last few years he's obviously been getting increasingly lonely.' She paused for a moment, then smiled shyly at Sylvia and looked up at her from under her thick lashes. 'You've been incredible,' she said, 'absolutely incredible. I'll never be able to thank you enough for all you've done for him.'

Sylvia thought, 'Steady on!' but said nothing.

'I can really tell he's fond of you,' Jocelyn went on. 'You can have no idea how glad I am,' she paused again and looked straight at Sylvia and held her gaze. 'You see, up to now all his affection has been centred on me – rather too much so.' Another pause.

Sylvia suddenly felt that the silence was ominous. She wasn't sure that she wanted to hear any more.

'You obviously understand the problems,' Jocelyn sighed, 'I mean the drink – it's a real problem. I think it's probably getting worse if anything – last night, for instance, was really bad. And thank you, Sylvia, you were wonderful. I don't know what I would have done without you.'

Sylvia remembered Jocelyn standing there in the hall, staring coldly at her father's unconscious body as it was dragged across the floor. Sylvia couldn't make head or tail of what was going on. 'Well, never mind,' she said fatuously, 'it's all over now.' She knew, of course, that it wasn't, but she was beginning to wish that Jocelyn would spit out whatever it was she'd come to say and just go away. She looked anxiously at her watch and realised that it would soon be time for the ten o'clock news and for her mother to go to bed and for Wilf to arrive. Then she remembered that she had left the door unlocked when she let Jocelyn in. She could hardly go back and lock it now, which meant that Hardcastle would probably come bursting in at any moment. She wondered fleetingly what had happened to her dull old life.

Jocelyn remained firmly on the sofa. She had absolutely no intention of moving until she had said what it was that she had come to say.

'You see, I'm really dreadfully worried about Dad,' Jocelyn went determinedly on. 'He obviously drinks

because he can't face up to what he's done, and I feel –
no, honestly I do – that if he were ever made to look at
what he's done, it could be the end of him. He could
kill himself.'

'How would you feel about that?' Sylvia suddenly
asked, rather sharply, surprising herself almost as much
as Jocelyn by the pertinence of the question.

Jocelyn was thrown for a moment. She hadn't made
any provision for that kind of comeback. She ran her
hand through her hair again whilst wondering how to
cope with it. 'Poor Dad,' she eventually said rather
feebly, 'it would be terrible.'

Sylvia really wanted to confront this girl, who was
sitting there so impertinently and so inconveniently on
her sofa and to ask her what it was she wanted and why
she had come, but something about Jocelyn forbade any
further intrusion.

'I couldn't tell anyone – not anyone,' Jocelyn went
on, 'about Dad and me – what he did to me – I mean,
poor Dad, he might even have to go to prison . . .'

Sylvia opened her mouth to speak but couldn't think
what to say. She felt she must say something on being
told of this appalling crime – but what? It could all be
true, she'd believe almost anything of Hardcastle, but
Jocelyn reeked of deceit, sitting there so prettily on the
sofa, so the whole thing could equally well be a pack of
lies. Sylvia had come to this house as a simple housekeeper such a short while ago and now everything
seemed to have got out of hand all at once.

Lady Field, who had been sitting there knitting,
apparently impervious to what was going on, suddenly
turned round and looked down her nose haughtily at
Jocelyn. She was quite furious with the little hussy and
thought that she had perfectly understood the girl's
game. She had realised from the very start that hers and

Jocelyn's interests were directly opposed, but she would never have dreamed that the girl would go so far as to invent such lies about her own father just to prevent Sylvia from marrying him. It was disgraceful what people would think up these days. Personally, she didn't believe in all this abuse – it was just got up by the media to titillate the public. In any case, it was quite ridiculous to suppose that anything of the sort could happen in a family like the Hardcastles'. The girl needed to be spoken to severely. But more importantly, she should be got out of the room and Sylvia should be prevented from believing a word of it. Then again, if Hardcastle had got up to a little hanky-panky who could blame him, all alone without a wife – and with that daughter, who was obviously a little siren. Men, Lady Field knew, were notoriously weak where that kind of thing was concerned.

It was getting late and Lady Field realised to her annoyance that they had missed the beginning of the news. She folded up her knitting and determinedly stuck a ball of pink wool on the end of the needles.

'You young people,' she said, 'may well like sitting up until all hours of the night, but it's my bedtime and Sylvia's, and I'm afraid that the time has come for you to go home.' She turned to her daughter, 'Sylvia, dear, would you mind getting your mother a hot-water bottle?'

Jocelyn had done what she came to do and despite the rather flat reaction to her story, she felt sure that it must have taken root. When Sylvia thought about it later she would surely be horrified and any intention she had of marrying Hardcastle would be forgotten. It was a shame that Lady Field hadn't been more shocked, Jocelyn would have liked to think of her banging home the horror of the situation to Sylvia. Jocelyn hated

Sylvia. She hated her gentle manner and her look of calm composure, but above all she hated her for having her eye on Hardcastle. Hardcastle belonged to Jocelyn.

'Thanks for the coffee,' she said, standing up, 'and thanks for letting me come and talk. It was sweet of you,' she smiled at Sylvia, but didn't bother with Lady Field. 'I'm so sorry if I kept you up – I'd no idea how late it was.'

Despite her appearance of calm composure, Sylvia was feeling anything but calm. Prophecy was lying in the doorway, wagging her tail and looking up longingly at her mistress as though to reproach her for neglect, but Sylvia could think only of how to get rid of Jocelyn – she didn't even have time at the moment to dwell on the awful things she had just been told. That would come later: now she must lock that interconnecting door as soon as possible and see her mother off to bed so as to be ready to welcome Wilf who, she was quite certain, would not let her down. Her mouth was dry and she felt very, very tense.

'Oh, Prophecy!' she exclaimed impatiently, 'do get out of the way.' Prophecy just rolled over onto her back and waved her paws in the air, delighted at last to have attracted attention.

Sylvia couldn't resist the temptation to bend down and pat her beloved dog and just as she did so she heard the doorbell ring and, at the same time, there was a terrific clattering noise in the kitchen and Hardcastle's voice was heard bawling angrily, 'Where is she? Where's my daughter? Jocelyn!'

X

The night that Milly went back to work Evidence slept badly, which was unusual for him. He supposed that all this infernal fuss stirred up about his father by Gatey was at the root of the matter and so he spent a large part of the night thinking about Gatey, wishing her to be more relaxed or less emotional and rationalising his own position. On the whole, Evidence's position was quite simple and was based entirely on self-protection. In fact he didn't trust himself ever to display any emotion, although he might not have put it exactly like that himself. He would have said that he wanted to protect Milly or that nothing he could do at this late stage could possibly help his father, who had quite simply chosen his own path. He might occasionally have paused to say, 'Poor thing', but beyond that his involvement ceased.

Evidence had to get on with his own life. He did not want his father to intrude on it and neither, for that matter, did he want his mother to. When Evidence thought about her he always felt slightly suffocated and that feeling of suffocation was so uncomfortable that he immediately turned away from it and thought of something else.

As he lay sleepless that night the problem of his father assumed gigantic proportions, as even the slightest problems do in the small hours. What in God's name were they to do if they found him? Then he thought that they wouldn't – couldn't – find him. It would be so unlikely, quite impossible, like a needle in a haystack – a tramp in a haystack . . . For a moment he dozed off and dreamed of rows and rows of tramps asleep, like Little Boy Blue, at the bottom of a haystack. But he soon woke again. What would he do with this tramp in the awful event of him being found? He couldn't come to live with Evidence and Milly. That would be completely out of the question and there was nowhere else where he could go, so he would just have to go back on the streets and continue his life as a tramp – a gentleman of the road. It was a way of life which he had chosen for himself and which, for all Evidence knew, he had come to like, to be at home with. Frederick had never been very happy before, when he was a clergyman – a so-called respected member of society. Perhaps it suited him better to be a tramp.

Whilst trying to rationalise his position and to convince himself that he had no moral responsibility for his father, Evidence also felt angry and ashamed. How could his father ever have descended to such depths and, furthermore, how dared he have done so? Evidence wondered if he would have even recognised Frederick if he had passed him in the street. He sincerely hoped that he would never have to see him again and then began to wonder what it was about Gatey – or about Frederick – that made Gatey so concerned for him. Then he began to feel angry with Gatey for wanting to stir everything up, for not being prepared to leave well alone.

Next, images of his drunken father invading the

cleanness of his and Milly's home began to haunt him. Milly, he feared, would be too tolerant; there Frederick would be when Evidence came home from work, sitting on the sofa drooling on about Nietzsche – or blue whales – or whatever nonsense was preoccupying him at the moment. He realised with disgust that by now his father's brain must be truly sozzled with drink and that there could be no hope for him.

Eventually, in the early hours, he fell asleep and slept until Milly got back from work and woke him. As he crawled out of bed, bad-tempered and bleary-eyed, and went to have a shower, he felt irritable and worried that he might be late for work. He came back into the bedroom where Milly, weary from her night's work, lay on the unmade bed and talked to him. She wished that circumstances could be more favourable and even wondered if she ought to wait until the evening to break the news, but that would be just as difficult, or even worse, because Evidence would be tired and she would be hurrying off to work. She wished she wasn't on night-duty.

Evidence was standing at the end of the bed drying himself on a ridiculously small, lemon-yellow towel. He was extremely handsome, but as Milly looked at his bony, white body, she suddenly saw him as completely absurd. There was a particular absurdity in the concentration with which he dried his armpits and in the tension and irritation which seemed to animate his whole being. Milly supposed she was tired, but for a moment everything suddenly seemed to be too much for her.

She thought of the bearded, worn-out man in the hospital bed, drooling on about God and poetry and for a moment even he seemed more substantial than the thin, golden god standing there at the end of the bed

148

drying himself so seriously with that silly little towel, and whom she loved.

'Evidence,' she said, 'this may not be the right moment, but I'm afraid that there is something which I have to tell you.'

Evidence grunted and went on thinking about how annoying it was to have overslept.

'We can talk about it this evening,' he said.

Milly jumped off the bed and walked towards him. He was buttoning his shirt with the same absurd air of concentration.

'It's important,' she said. 'It can't wait. Look, it's about your father. I'm sorry, I really am, but it's not my fault. Do you know where he is? He's in the hospital – in my ward – lying there with pneumonia, poor fellow. I've just left him.'

Evidence suddenly stopped concentrating on what he was doing and looked at Milly and was startled by the intensity of her expression. He was overwhelmed with irritation. How dared she come and tell him all this nonsense now, just as he was getting dressed and when he had overslept and was going to be late for work? He had no time to listen. Why wasn't she in the kitchen making the coffee – couldn't she see that he was in a hurry?

'For God's sake,' he snapped as he zipped up his trousers, 'where are my socks? I can't talk about my father now.' In fact, he hadn't really taken in what Milly had been saying, which was indeed the very stuff of his nightmares.

Milly didn't know what to do. 'I'll go and put the kettle on,' she said.

When Evidence joined her in the kitchen a few minutes later the full horror of what he had been told was just beginning to sink in.

'Did you tell him who you were?' he asked.

'No,' said Milly, 'I wanted to tell you first. He's not at all well, he'll be there for a few days.'

It crossed Evidence's mind to wonder if his father were dying. That would be one solution.

'I've no idea what to do,' he said, 'but he can't come here. Do you understand? I won't have it!'

'I'll write to Gatey,' Milly said. 'Or with a bit of luck she may telephone first.'

Gatey did telephone later that morning, just as Milly had dropped off to sleep, but Milly didn't mind because she was so relieved to have someone to talk to about the problem. She wished so desperately that Evidence would show some signs of responsibility towards his father, although in a way she couldn't see how any of them were really going to be able to help Frederick. She hated the way that Evidence just stated categorically that his father was not to come to their house. It seemed most unlikely to Milly that a man who had been living rough for so long would suddenly want to settle down in a middle-class, suburban estate with his estranged son. All the same, it would be only charitable to offer him a roof over his head until he felt strong enough to return to his own way of life, which now it would probably be impossible for him to give up. Milly had seen men like Frederick before.

When Gatey heard that her father had turned up she was enormously excited.

'I had a feeling in my bones that we'd find him in the end,' she squeaked. 'How is he? What does he look like? Why didn't you tell him who you were?' she asked breathlessly.

Gatey would be in Manchester again by the evening, with any luck before Evidence was even back from work.

'We'll go together to see Dad,' she said.

Milly doubted that Evidence would be prepared to go.

Gatey was appalled. She knew Evidence was a pig, but she didn't think he could be quite such a pig as that.

'What'll we tell Mum?' Gatey wanted to know.

'You and Evidence will have to decide on that,' said Milly. 'Think about it on the way up – I must get some sleep – see you this evening . . .'

But, like Evidence, Milly was unable to sleep. She was haunted by the sad, lined face on the hospital pillow. She wondered what Frederick was really like – or what he would have been like had he not allowed alcohol to rot his brain. For her he had always been some sort of mythical character about whom she received such conflicting messages from Gatey and from Evidence. She worried about the effect Frederick would have on Gatey, whose imagination had certainly been working on her memory of her father. So for that matter, in quite a different way, had Evidence's.

Gatey was beside herself with excitement at the prospect of seeing her father again and very slightly delighted by the circumstances themselves. She did not wonder what he would be like after all these years nor did it occur to her to think that he might have deteriorated mentally since she had last seen him. She romanticised him and somehow managed to forget the worst aspects of his drunkenness and weakness of character which had wreaked such misery on her childhood.

As she hitched her way back to Manchester she imagined some kind of Hollywood reunion in which the reality of her father played no part, since it never occurred to her to imagine what his state of mind might truly be. She was all ready to carry him back to London to her squat where she would give him her bed and nurse him back to health. She didn't ask herself what would happen after that – where he would go or how he would spend his days. Neither did she doubt for a moment that he would want to come back to London with her. She was a combination of Mother Teresa and a knight on a white charger. The whole thing was incredibly romantic.

In hospital Frederick lay feverishly in bed, occasionally dozing off and wondering at intervals about the pretty nurse who had been on night-duty. He couldn't possibly have seen her before and yet there was something irritatingly familiar about her. When he had been on the road he had thought very little about the past, but now, in this clean bed in this bright ward his mind kept returning to those long-ago days when he had been an ordinary member of society and he thought of his wife and his children in a faintly sentimental way. His thoughts went back even further to his own childhood in a bishop's palace and to his father, lean and elegant in gaiters – a narcissistic man, dominated by a large and masculine wife. His mind swam and the bishop's palace of his childhood somehow became indistinguishable from the first rectory where he had lived with Sylvia. Then he thought of school and Oxford and theological college where he had trained for the Church. Strange pictures of the past came back to him with crystal clarity, whilst others remained more hazy – in all of them it was summertime. Frederick wondered if he was about to die and rather hoped he was. It would be an enormous relief.

A nurse had just brought him some pretty unappetising fish pie and carrots swimming in water when he noticed a funny little girl with cropped hair, dressed all in black, approaching his bed. He looked at the fish pie

and felt slightly sick; his hands were shaking uncontrol-
lably and what he really wanted was not fish pie but a
drink. He looked at the girl in black again and wondered
what she was doing there, smiling at the end of his bed.
She opened her mouth but nothing seemed to come out
and he wondered if she were just another figment of his
imagination, like the schoolmasters and rural deans and
other figures from the past who had come to haunt him
during the day.

The girl walked round to the side of the bed and
leaned over him. She gently removed the plate of fish
and this time he heard what she said. 'Yuck,' she said,
'how disgusting! Do they really expect you to eat that?'
Then he suddenly noticed that tears were streaming
down the girl's face.

'Dad,' she said, 'you don't even recognise me.'

Just as she spoke he realised that it was indeed Gatey,
but he was so ill and his mind was so confused that he
couldn't decide whether or not she was really a dream.
'Are you a dream?' he asked.

Gatey's picture of her reunion with her father could
not have been further removed from the reality. She
had certainly not accounted for the semi-delirious state
in which she found him and neither had she expected
him to be looking quite so old, or half so weak.
Suddenly the idea of him in the squat seemed rather
ridiculous. She thought her mother ought to look after
him. Or Evidence. Evidence had of course refused to
come to the hospital, despite the fact that Milly had
promised to reveal her identity as soon as she came on
night-duty. Milly had even dared to suggest that they
might harbour Frederick for a few convalescent days
when he came out of hospital. Evidence had turned
white at the suggestion and asked Milly what she
thought the social services were for.

Somewhere in his confusion Frederick felt over-whelmingly comforted by the presence of his daughter, which didn't appear to him to be at all surprising. In fact, it seemed quite normal that she should be sitting there beside him in hospital. And yet in the back of his mind there also lurked a faint feeling of fear which might, for all he knew, be connected with the approach of death.

Gatey simply didn't know what to say, which was odd because she was not usually at a loss for conversation.

Frederick was in a world of his own and didn't really feel the need to talk, so they remained there, silent, for a while and then he suddenly asked after Sylvia. 'I'd like to see your mother again,' he said.

There was a pause. Gatey had no idea whether or not her mother would be prepared, or even able, to come and see him. She couldn't think what to do.

'I saw your beastly old grandmother the other day,' he said with sudden clarity. 'In the street, here in Manchester. She hadn't changed much but it gave her quite a shock to see me.' He laughed a hollow, rasping laugh which developed into a fit of coughing and then a nurse appeared and told Gatey that she had been there long enough and that Mr Appleby was very tired and needed a rest.

When Milly came on duty later she found Frederick rather less well than he had been when she left him in the morning and so decided not to say anything about herself or Evidence. He was quite delirious and she wasn't at all sure that he would take in what she was saying. In a way she was relieved, as it postponed the need for any further action.

Frederick stayed in hospital for another five days by which time, although he was very weak, his temperature had been normal for three days. Gatey stayed with Milly and Evidence and came to see her father morning, afternoon and evening. On the second day she told him all about Evidence and Milly and how they were married and living in Manchester and how Milly had seen Frederick in the park a little while back, and she told him about her grandmother's horrible letter and about her search for her father. She reminisced about the olden days and reminded Frederick of how he had taken her out of school to go to Scotland and of his wild enthusiasms for kite flying and skating.

As Frederick became less delirious he listened intently to everything Gatey had to say. It still seemed perfectly normal that she should be there taking care of him, but he did not always like what she talked about. Reminiscence was dangerous ground, on which he often felt acutely uncomfortable and which sometimes sank him into unbearable depression and then he would long for a drink, but Gatey always refused to bring him any alcohol. He began, too, to become quite fond of Milly whom, after all, he had liked from the start, even before he knew who she was. He was frightened of the prospect of seeing Evidence and never asked about him. But he did ask about Sylvia. He wanted to know how she was, where she was, whether she was happy – lonely – married again . . .

Gatey gladly told him at length about her mother and where she lived and about Percy Hardcastle and what a monster he was and about Prophecy and about how Sylvia was all right really, but probably rather lonely.

Frederick wanted very badly to see Sylvia again. He loved her and had always refused to admit to himself the possibility that she did not return that love. Of course he knew that things had been difficult, he sometimes even allowed himself to think that his drunkenness was at fault, but at other times he produced endless, convoluted arguments to explain that away. Then he saw himself as an outsider who could never, and never could have conformed to society and who was somehow destined to be alone, to live as he did, which sometimes seemed to him to be the only possible and right way to live. Occasionally, when he felt very low, he still prayed, although he was not at all sure what it was he believed in or to whom it was he prayed. He was still a priest though, of that there could be no doubt. That was something which could never be taken away from him by the rural dean or the bishop or anyone else for that matter. And sometimes, even when he was in the gutter, he felt a pride in bearing this mantle of priesthood, which somehow confirmed his difference from other men and emphasised his aloneness, made him feel especially chosen by whatever god existed. Then of course he would feel overwhelmingly guilty at his betrayal of that priesthood and then he would need a drink, and another, and another.

The hospital social worker came to see Frederick to see what help he might need when he was discharged.

None, he said. He would go back to his old way of life, a way of life which in the end he had chosen. The social worker went away, relieved that she had done her duty, but wondering at the back of her mind just how long the poor fellow could last. She did not doubt that he would be back on the bottle within hours of leaving hospital. When she had asked him gently if he had ever thought of going to Alcoholics Anonymous, he had merely replied with a mild guffaw. She reminded him that he was probably feeling better and clearer-headed now than he had done for a very long time and asked him if he wouldn't like to go on feeling better.

'There's more to it than that,' he said, and she went away.

By the end of five days Milly felt that she was on the verge of persuading Evidence to allow his father to come and stay for a day or two immediately after leaving hospital. She thought that if he did eventually agree she would have performed a miracle. She and Gatey between them.

She explained that Frederick was absolutely not aggressive, that in fact he was meek and mild and, since he had stopped bellowing for drink, a very amenable patient. If he were to come they would give him no alcohol and they would warn him quite firmly that he could only stay for a very short while. Gatey and she were united in their reforming zeal and in their determination not to turn Frederick out onto the streets.

Evidence hadn't been sleeping at all since hearing that his father had turned up and as the days went by his dread of meeting Frederick again increased drastically. The whole thing was completely monstrous. He had nothing to say to his father and only unhappy memories of him. Memories of humiliation and shame, anger and bitterness, none of which he felt the least inclined to forgive, besides, he felt that he was more worldly-wise than Milly or Gatey. Neither of them seemed to realise that by having Frederick to stay for two days they were merely adding insult to the injury of eventually turning him back onto the streets. Evidence also felt quite convinced that Frederick's behaviour would alter as soon as he left hospital and that somehow, by hook or by crook, he would manage to get hold of some alcohol and then the whole nightmare would only become worse. Gatey must have forgotten what he had been like.

Oh, no she hadn't. But she, unlike her brother, had

hope and faith in the possibility of change. So there were Milly and Gatey with their pure, eager faces begging for mercy. How in the long run could Evidence refuse their request, particularly when it would result in people being able to say, 'Evidence Appleby threw his dying father out onto the streets.' That did not sound very pretty and somewhere in his heart he realised that it wasn't very nice either. But part of him wished that his father had died and part of him went on thinking that if he were only half a man he would refuse to bow to these foolish women. No good would come of it – in fact it would be completely pointless, just a sop to all their consciences.

'Not at all,' said Milly rather pompously. 'He's already told the hospital social worker that he chose his way of life and that he intends to return to it . . .'

'Chose his way of life – bloody drunk,' said Evidence, but he knew that in the end he would probably give in. He felt sick and couldn't eat and he himself wanted a drink. He pounded up and down the sitting-room, his hands plunged into his pockets. In a minute he would ask Gatey for a roll-up – he couldn't stand any more of this.

Milly felt so relieved when she set out to work that evening, knowing that at last she would be able to extend an invitation to her father-in-law even though she rather dreaded the days he would be spending with them and could perfectly well see that the whole episode might be most awfully embarrassing and even, to a certain extent, pointless. But at least Frederick would be that little bit stronger by the time he took to the road again.

She wondered how Evidence would cope with seeing his father – surely he would find it easier than he imagined. It occurred to her that the situation might be rather more difficult for Frederick than for Evidence. He hadn't enquired once about his son, in fact he had barely referred to him in any of his conversations with Gatey or Milly, except perhaps once or twice to make some slightly disparaging remark, half jokingly, which they had both ignored. Gatey had told Milly that, much as she loved her father, she thought he had been particularly hard on Evidence when they all lived together, putting him down a lot and getting very angry with him for no reason. Gatey supposed that he had been a bit jealous of his son, who always succeeded quite well in what he set out to do and who showed every sign of being in complete control of his life.

Frederick had frequently found himself slightly irritated by Evidence's lack of humour and by what he saw as his straight-laced priggishness, and he was irritated, too, by the boy's tall, good looks – as if good looks had anything to do with anything. And Sylvia had always had an annoying way of sticking up for her son, ever since he was a child, as if he were a little weakling and unable to stand up for himself. Where was Sylvia's loyalty? She should have been standing up for Frederick.

There was no doubt about it that Frederick had taken to Milly, who was a pretty, kind girl, and straightforward, too, but he didn't care to discuss Evidence with her and was glad that she showed no inclination to talk about him, either. Perhaps Milly didn't like her husband very much. Frederick wouldn't be at all surprised – Evidence had always struck him as rather a cold sort of fellow.

Frederick dozed on and off and wondered how long they would let him stay in hospital. He felt much better than he had done a day or two ago and was even beginning to tolerate the lack of alcohol and, besides, it was quite comfortable in the ward, with all these nurses and doctors to take care of you and with regular meals as well. He felt rather exhausted at the prospect of taking to the streets again and wished that he had died. There was nothing left to live for, he knew that now and the time was ripe. He was glad he had had the chance to see Gatey again but he didn't suppose that he would get another one once he had left the hospital. He wondered if the weather had got any warmer during the few days he had been off the streets. He fell asleep again and when he woke Milly was standing by his bed, smiling.

Despite her smiling face he wished he had woken in heaven – or hell. He had no strength for the cold, bleak streets and public lavatories any more.

'Frederick,' said Milly, taking his hand, 'we don't know yet when the doctor's going to discharge you, but I expect it may be any day now and when it does happen Evidence and I would like you to come and stay with us for a little while.' At the last moment her courage failed her and she could not bring herself to say anything which sounded so mean as 'for two nights', which was what she had promised Evidence she would say. Instead she substituted 'for a little while'.

'Gatey will go back to London,' she said, 'and you could have the spare room.'

Frederick felt completely stunned. It was a very long time since he had heard any mention of spare rooms, let alone entertained the idea of actually staying in one. He wondered what it would be like and began to imagine endless nights of blissful, uninterrupted sleep in clean sheets.

'Frederick,' said Milly gently, leaning over him, 'are you all right? Did you hear what I said?'

'You are both very kind,' he said tonelessly.

Then a patient from across the ward called for a nurse and Milly had to hurry away. 'I'll come back and see you later,' she said over her shoulder to her father-in-law. 'We really want you to come.'

The ward was under-staffed and the rest of the night was dreadfully busy, with one patient dying and another being hurried to occupy his bed and another burst an aorta and had to be rushed down two floors to have an emergency operation. Just before she left in the morning Milly went to have a word with Frederick, who had had his breakfast and dozed off again. He sensed her presence and half opened his eyes.

'Take care,' she said quietly. 'See you this evening – and remember what I said. We're looking forward to having you.'

As Frederick watched Milly disappearing down the ward he thought about spare bedrooms and pink wallpaper and clean finger nails and polite conversation and waiting to be offered a drink, and he thought in a bleary way how far he had travelled and what a gulf there was between him and them. He thought about Evidence and couldn't imagine what he was like now and couldn't imagine what it would be like being in his house. Evidence, he imagined, might be a bit of a bore – a prig – rather disapproving, probably. He wondered if he kept any drink in his house.

Later that day Frederick discharged himself from hospital. When Milly came on duty that night she found his bed was empty.

XI

Jocelyn was angry. In the event she resorted to overt
blackmail and as soon as she had extracted the cheque
she needed from her father, she ordered a taxi for the
station and headed back to London. She supposed that
after everything that had happened there could no
longer be any possibility of that woman wanting to
marry her father, or vice versa. For her own part she
decided that getting money out of her father was too
difficult and unpleasant, involving her as it did in these
unpleasant trips to the country and in unbearable closeness to her father. Her thoughts turned to the rich
young lord and she decided that he might well be worth
going for after all.

Sylvia was thankful to have Jocelyn out of the way.
That meant one person at least who wouldn't be causing
any more trouble, for the moment at any rate, although
Hardcastle was ranting like a bull about his daughter's
departure and about how she only used him – only
came to see him for what she could get out of him.
Sylvia thought that that was probably true, as she had
formed a very unfavourable opinion of Jocelyn
altogether. What she still couldn't quite make out was

precisely why Jocelyn had decided to come and tell her those awful things about Hardcastle the evening before. She had absolutely no way of knowing whether Jocelyn had been speaking the truth or not and no idea what, if anything, she should do about the information. She could try to forget that she had ever heard it. That would probably be the best thing, but it was all so hauntingly unpleasant that with the best will in the world, it would be particularly difficult to expunge from her consciousness. Quite apart from all that she couldn't get last night's awful scene out of her head.

There had been her mother, in the background, standing tut-tutting and smugly putting her knitting away in a horrid mock-tapestry bag. She herself had been bending down to pat Prophecy as Jocelyn strode past her haughtily and stepped over the dog to confront her hopelessly drunk father, whilst Wilf had been outside banging at the door expecting a quiet chat and a nightcap.

Everything was quite out of control. It was as if all Sylvia's nightmares had conspired to bedevil her at the same time. The first thing she had done was to open the door to Wilf, thereby providing herself with an ally, but at the same time putting the cat among the pigeons.

Wilf took one look at the scene as he came through the door and said to Jocelyn, 'If I were you, I'd take your old man back next door.'

Jocelyn turned a scornful look on Wilf and told him to mind his own business, whilst Hardcastle pointed a furious finger at him and asked what that little so-and-so was doing here again. Then Lady Field had joined in, twittering on about manners and no one having any respect for her these days.

'I'm going to bed,' she said firmly, but the doorway was blocked, so she just had to stand there, holding her horrid tapestry bag and looking furious. 'Well,' she said, 'I shall go to bed if anyone will have the courtesy to allow me to pass. And tomorrow I think I shall return to Manchester where people are more civilised.'

Sylvia wasn't at all sure what had happened next but she vaguely remembered Wilf clearing a passage for Lady Field and ushering her out of the room. Then Hardcastle and Jocelyn began to shout abuse at each other in the most unrestrained fashion. Suddenly Sylvia put both her hands to her ears and just said, 'Please, please go! Go and talk to each other next door.' Then she pushed them both gently in the direction she wanted them to go, and said she was sorry.

'Don't you dare touch me!' Jocelyn snapped at her, attempting as she did so to brush Sylvia's hand away.

Then Hardcastle had said something appalling about marrying Sylvia and Sylvia, despite her years, had blushed and very nearly cried and Jocelyn had replied with a sneer, 'I wouldn't count on it if I were you,' and, with a nod in Wilf's direction, 'She prefers the rough trade here.' Then she had stalked out of the room, followed by her father, who was gabbling on incoherently about love and marriage and fine women and ungrateful children.

When at last they had gone, Wilf drew the bolt on the interconnecting door.

'I thought you were going to keep this locked,' he said.

'I was,' said Sylvia, 'but I forgot. Have a drop of whisky,' she added. 'I've got some and I reckon we need it.'

'I don't think you really ought to stay here,' Wilf said, 'with all that going on. It's not very nice for you.'

They were sitting as usual at the kitchen table. Sylvia

looked long and hard straight at Wilf. 'I don't want to leave,' she said.

Wilf lowered his glance; he looked at his drink and twiddled his glass round nervously on the table. The hooded look came over his face.

'I can cope with drunks,' she said bluntly. 'I told you, I was married to one. At least I'm not married to Mr Hardcastle . . .' She laughed awkwardly. 'I'll be perfectly all right if I can only remember to lock that blasted door.'

Wilf silently wished that he could ask Sylvia to come and live with him and tried to imagine her in his little bungalow. He wondered how they would manage; would it be too close quarters – were they too old for such a change? Would she look down on him? Let her dare.

'I never told you that my husband was a clergyman, did I?' Sylvia asked suddenly.

Wilf looked at her and laughed. 'A parson's wife!' he said and, not too unkindly, 'I might have guessed it.'

Sylvia felt piqued, as she almost always did at any reaction to her being a clergyman's wife. 'That may not surprise you,' she said sharply, 'but I can guarantee that the clergyman in question would.' Then, although she would have liked Wilf to know about her life, she felt a great wave of exhaustion and no longer wanted to talk about Frederick – to think about Frederick – to know that Frederick ever existed. It was as though Frederick had taken the best of her and left the husk to rot by the wayside.

'I don't really want to talk about Frederick,' she said. 'I'll tell you about him one day though, I expect.'

There was a pause. 'Would you say,' Wilf began with the firm intention of changing the subject and causing a small stir, 'that a man hadn't lived if he had never been to gaol?'

'I can't say I've ever thought about it quite like that,' she said and then added, rather nervously, 'Why? Have you been to prison?'

'It was a long time ago,' he said.

Over the past few weeks Sylvia had learnt a lot about Wilf's life as they sat talking round her kitchen table, but this was the first time she had heard about him going to prison. To begin with the news gave her an uncomfortable feeling of dread. What on earth had he done? She knew that his mother had died when he was only a child, that he had never known his father and had been sent to live with a bad-tempered aunt who already had too many children of her own, whilst his brother, whom Wilf never saw or heard of again, went into a children's home. When Wilf was fifteen he ran away from the bad-tempered aunt, lied about his age and joined the Merchant Navy and so saw a bit of the world. Glad to have done it, but in his opinion there was no place like England. And nothing to beat the South Downs.

It wasn't until he was nearly thirty, when he met his wife, that Wilf began to settle down, but it all took some time and would probably have taken longer if his wife hadn't insisted that they move out of London, away from Wilf's old haunts.

He was a bit wild in those days and used to get violent; he beat up a policeman a couple of times and that's what he'd been inside for – twice. To this day he dreamed about it. Occasionally he woke up in a panic, hearing those doors lock behind him and terrified of going back. He was very lucky that it hadn't turned out that way.

Sylvia's heart went out to Wilf, but he gave a bitter laugh.

'It was years ago now,' he said.

All of a sudden, as they sat chatting, Sylvia heard the floorboards overhead creaking.

'Oh Lord!' she said, 'I'd completely forgotten about my mother – she's walking about upstairs.'

Then they heard her footsteps on the stairs. A moment later she burst into the kitchen.

'I came down to make myself a cup of tea,' said Lady Field. 'I couldn't sleep as a result of that terrible kerfuffle. People are so selfish these days. In my young day there would have been some respect shown to an elderly person. I haven't noticed any respect around these parts, I must say. And Sylvia, what on earth are you doing still up at this hour? You do get so dreadfully tired you know, you always have. You'll look pale and have rings under your eyes.' She turned a baleful glance on Wilf, 'And I can't think what you're always doing here,' she remarked icily. 'Especially at this time of night. Don't you have a home of your own to go to?'

Suddenly Sylvia was enraged. Wilf had taken enough insults for one evening – and all of them provoked by simple class snobbery. She felt she would like to run away with Wilf for the sheer pleasure of annoying her mother. Perhaps it was the whisky which loosened her tongue, but no one was more surprised than she when she heard herself speak.

'We were talking about prison,' she said. 'Wilf has been telling me what it's like inside.'

As soon as she spoke she realised that she was making a terrible mistake and then there was an ominous silence. It was quite unlike Sylvia to act so rashly.

Lady Field broke the silence. 'I suppose I shouldn't be surprised to see the parson's wife keeping company with the gaolbird,' she said. She didn't really know precisely what she meant by that but she was very angry indeed. There was a further silence while she clattered around, boiling the kettle and making herself a cup of tea and then, without anyone uttering another word, she left the room.

Sylvia could only apologise to Wilf. She couldn't think what had possessed her, if not a desire to shock her mother.

'It doesn't matter,' said Wilf. But it clearly did. It had been a dreadful evening and everyone had said things they would regret. 'I'd better be going,' he said coldly. 'Be seeing you,' and he got up and left – disappeared in to the dark of the night.

Sylvia sat on for a while at the kitchen table, her head sunk in her hands, large, hot tears rolling down her cheeks. What a muddle! What a dreadful muddle! She had a horrible feeling that from now onwards Wilf would keep his distance. He had looked pretty grim when he left and who could blame him, when she had just abused his confidence in the stupidest possible way? She could understand if he didn't feel like coming back.

As the tears rolled and rolled down her cheeks she went over and over the evening in her mind, over all the ghastly, horrible things which had been said and for the first time for a long time, she wished she didn't have to wake up in the morning. Then she began to wonder if she could rectify the situation in any way. Perhaps she could tell her mother that it was a joke – that it wasn't true. But would her mother believe her? Sylvia thought not. Despite her anger, there had been a grim satisfaction in Lady Field's acknowledgement of the information and only Sylvia knew quite how much her mother cherished any unpleasant piece of news which she felt might come in handy as a weapon sometime. What on earth had got into Sylvia to allow her to speak so? And even if Lady Field did believe that Sylvia had made it up on the spur of the moment, she would never let it rest. And what about Wilf? How could he face her again? It was perfectly obvious that he didn't want a thing like that gossiped about and passed around. He would surely never trust her again and would probably think she was just a silly, talkative, middle-aged woman. Sometimes Sylvia thought that there was something in her which caused her to do the very thing which would most harm her own interests. Look what a mess she had made of her life. Her marriage – her children – everything. What was the matter with her? Why was she living in this horrid bit of a house, working for an offensive drunk? 'Oh God,' she wept. 'Oh my God!' How had she dared to suppose that a little happiness had at last come her way in the shape of Wilf? What a fool she had been – what a damned fool.

Wilf was just a lonely man who liked a cup of tea and a chat – how had she dared to delude herself that there was any more to it than that? She felt a fool – a dreadful, dreadful fool and turned as she always did to Prophecy for comfort. Prophecy jumped up and put her paws on Sylvia's lap and began to lick away her tears. Sylvia put her arms around Prophecy's massive head and dissolved into fresh tears.

By the time Sylvia eventually went to bed she was completely worn out, her nose was blocked and her eyes were swollen.

So in the morning there was Hardcastle, ranting like a bull because his darling daughter had flown the nest, but not for the moment talking about marrying Sylvia. Sylvia felt terrible as she prepared his breakfast and even began to wonder if she shouldn't marry the brute as a sort of self-punishment. She didn't deserve anything better, she decided.

Lady Field came down in fighting form. She had decided not to go back to Manchester.

'Well,' she said as she ate her cornflakes – she always liked her cornflakes – 'What a to-do, I must say. Fancy my daughter going for a gaolbird! I can't imagine what your father would have said.'

Sylvia was sitting beside her mother, not eating a piece of toast and marmalade which lay uninvitingly on her plate.

'I don't know what you mean,' she said feebly.

'I don't suppose you know what I mean either when I say that Frederick was a drunk?' said Lady Field.

'Oh do let's just leave Frederick out of it, shall we?' Sylvia said irritably.

Lady Field took a large mouthful of cornflakes which she munched slowly before adding, 'I saw him the other day.'

'Saw who?' Sylvia asked dully.

'Frederick, of course,' said Lady Field. 'Who else? I'd hardly be talking about that little gaolbird of yours.'

'There's no need to be so offensive,' said Sylvia. She felt desperate and didn't know whether or not to defend Wilf or to turn her attention to this new, somewhat disturbing news about Frederick. She decided to say no more. She couldn't bear to hear anything about Frederick from her mother and neither could she bear even to give her mother the satisfaction of surprising her or engaging her interest.

'I would have thought you might have been interested in what I was saying,' Lady Field said after a while.

'Frederick has nothing to do with me any more,' Sylvia said harshly, 'so why should I concern myself

with his whereabouts?' In her heart she suddenly longed
to know that he was alive and all right – at least sort of
all right.

'I have to say that he was looking pretty awful,' Lady
Field continued. 'Pass the teapot, will you dear?'

Sylvia felt like chucking the teapot at her.

'He's living in Manchester, of course,' said Lady
Field.

Sylvia's curiosity was naturally aroused but she was
determined not to play the game. She jumped up. 'I
must go,' she said. 'I've got things to do next door.'
And she made a dash for it, out of the frying pan into
the fire.

'I ought to warn you,' Hardcastle said as she appeared
in his kitchen, 'against that little fellow Wapshott. I
wouldn't trust him if I were you.'

'You seem to trust him enough to employ him,' she
retorted.

'I wasn't talking about trusting him financially,'
Hardcastle leered.

Sylvia felt quite sick and began to wonder if she
really could put up with any more of this kind of thing.
But where – if she were to leave – would she go?
Immediately now she had to take the loose covers off in
the sitting-room and put them in the washing machine.
When she had done that she decided that she would
make herself pretty scarce for the rest of the day, not
that she relished the thought of spending the time with
her mother, in her present mood.

She thought she had made a mess of everything; she
seemed even to have wasted her resources. Years ago
there were so many things she had loved doing but
now she just dragged herself round, did what she had
to do and was left with no energy for anything else at
all. She used to paint a bit and garden and read a lot.

She hadn't painted or even picked up a paintbrush for years and of course she hadn't got a garden any more, but why was it that she only read trash – sometimes the same trash, over and over again? She couldn't remember when she had last read anything really worth reading. And now with no Wilf she might as well be dead.

To Sylvia's relief Lady Field announced in the middle of the morning that all yesterday evening's fuss had been too much for her; she was feeling so out of sorts that she would have to go back to bed for the rest of the day. Sylvia prepared a poached egg on toast for her mother's lunch, which she laid neatly on a tray and carried up to her bedroom, where it was spurned, declared to be over-cooked and sent away again. Sylvia threw the egg disgustedly into the bin and retired to her own bed with an old Dick Francis and Prophecy.

'You and Dick Francis,' she said to Prophecy, 'you're all that makes life worth living.' She wished Wilf would come and see her.

That very evening as she prepared his supper, Hardcastle came ranting into the kitchen, apparently less drunk than usual, but just as bellicose. He had had a telephone call from Jocelyn.

'Not a word about it while she was here!' he bawled. 'Not a bloody word, and now as soon as she gets back to London she comes out with this!'

Sylvia wondered what on earth could possibly have happened so suddenly.

'She wants to get married – can you believe it?' Hardcastle slumped down into a chair, rubbed his face in his hands and ruffled his hair. 'Why didn't she tell me?'

Sylvia couldn't answer that one, but she suggested that it might be a good thing. Perhaps it would make

Jocelyn happy, she hadn't seemed particularly happy to Sylvia.

'Why should she be happy?' Hardcastle suddenly barked.

'Oh I don't know,' said Sylvia feebly, 'a pretty girl like her – you can always hope.'

Hardcastle was perfectly furious. 'Pretty!' he yelled. 'Jocelyn's not pretty, she's beautiful.' He paused and then added, 'She wants an enormous wedding. Must think I'm made of money – but she knows I won't refuse.'

Sylvia thought it rather odd that no mention had yet been made of the bridegroom. 'Have you met the young man?' she asked.

'No,' Hardcastle said sadly. 'Never even heard of him until half an hour ago. Some sort of lord apparently – no job – lots of money. I don't know why he can't pay for the wedding. Sylvia,' Hardcastle looked at her pleadingly, 'what am I to do? She wants a great tent and dancing and five hundred people, and champagne, and a wedding dress to be made by some fancy fashion house in London – and God knows what else. I've just given her a lot of money – there isn't a bottomless pit.'

'Just say no,' said Sylvia. 'Tell her what you can afford and let her get on with it.' She looked at Hardcastle and caught his eye and in that fleeting moment she saw something that she hadn't seen there before – fear. Then she knew that he couldn't refuse his daughter anything and she knew the reason; what Jocelyn had told her about her father must be true. Hardcastle's gaze faltered as though he, too, in a moment of truth, had realised that Sylvia had read his mind.

Sylvia felt a momentary wave of pity at the sight of

Hardcastle rumbled, but it was immediately superseded by an even greater wave of disgust.

'I had my mind on quite a different marriage,' he said mournfully.

Sylvia shuddered inadvertently and by way of explanation remarked that the temperature had suddenly dropped. Out of the corner of her eye she saw Hardcastle still slumped over the table with his head buried in his hands. She stirred the soup and neither of them said anything for a while. She was thinking that he wasn't actually drunk and that this might be the right moment in which to explain once and for all that she had no intention of marrying him. She couldn't remember what kind of thing people were supposed to say under the circumstances and, besides, she felt acutely embarrassed and rather silly. She felt herself blush horribly as she suddenly wondered if she had imagined the whole thing about him wanting to marry her, or, if it was true, whether he had forgotten that he'd suggested it at all. Then she remembered Jocelyn shouting about the rough trade and last night's dreadful scene in all its ghastly detail and she knew that she must say something.

She turned to look at Hardcastle. He hadn't moved.

'Percy,' she forced herself to say gently. She never wanted to call him that again.

He looked up and in his eyes she recognised the pleading look of a whipped dog.

Oh God, she thought, what am I supposed to say? Wasn't there something people said on these occasions about being flattered?

'I feel,' she said awkwardly, 'that I owe you some sort of explanation. Perhaps I didn't make myself quite clear . . .' This was hell. 'And of course I'm very flattered, but I must tell you that I will go on working here if you want me to, but I can never marry you.' She turned back to the soup and began to stir it frantically again, thankful to have said what she had to say, but dreading to look again into those pleading, hangdog eyes.

She was amazed by what she heard next.

'I think you're very wise,' Hardcastle said flatly. 'I'm sorry I embarrassed you.'

As she turned thankfully to put the soup on the table she looked again at Hardcastle and again felt an extraordinary mixture of disgust and pity.

'I want to talk about Jocelyn,' he said abruptly. 'She'll ruin me – I don't know what to do about her. Please help me.'

How could Sylvia possibly help him? 'Your supper's ready,' she said.

Hardcastle staggered to his feet. He suddenly looked very old.

'I'll get myself a drink,' he said. 'I feel I need one – to celebrate . . .' He laughed a mirthless laugh.

'Well, I'll be going now,' said Sylvia. 'Good-night.'

When she returned to her side of the house she locked the interconnecting door firmly, leaving Hardcastle to get drunk alone.

XII

Hardcastle, who appeared to be unusually busy, was out a good deal during the next few days and he and Sylvia saw remarkably little of each other, which, to Sylvia at least, was a relief. Lady Field alone was enough trouble, so that Sylvia sometimes felt herself lost in a labyrinth of abnegation, self-effacement and self-loathing all of which might, she feared, eventually lead to some kind of explosion. She counted the hours until her mother's departure when she would at last be able to relax, cry, scream and wonder what had happened to Wilf.

For her part Lady Field kept up the good work of putting down her daughter – keeping her firmly in her place so that Sylvia felt herself reduced to the status of a child, always trying to please her mother, to excuse herself and in some horrible kind of way, to agree. She despised herself because she hardly agreed with anything her mother thought and yet she heard herself saying that she did.

Sylvia wondered where she had gone wrong. She knew of no one else who was quite so dominated by their mother so late in life or who so feared their mother's disapproval.

'I sometimes wonder where I went wrong with you, dear,' Lady Field opined and then laughed loudly at her own outrageous behaviour. 'I don't suppose you think that's very funny,' she went on, 'but then you were never very good at laughing at yourself.'

Sylvia gritted her teeth. 'What would you like to do today?' she asked brightly. 'We could go for a walk, or do some shopping . . .'

'I don't know why it is,' said Lady Field, 'but I have noticed that you always hurry away whenever I mention Frederick. I think that at your age you ought to be able to face up to the truth, but that, of course, is something else which you have never been able to do – just like your father, I suppose. He had a great capacity for burying his head in the sand, whereas I have always faced up to things myself – but then I have always been told that I am a particularly courageous person. I can't think why – well perhaps I can really . . .'

Sylvia had heard it all before, over and over again, and she knew as well as she knew anything that there was no point whatsoever in any kind of confrontation. Lady Field's defences were so sure that she could ward off almost any attack by appearing to be puzzled, hurt or misunderstood. As soon as the enemy showed the first sign of disarray, Lady Field brought up the rearguard and whammed in with a counter-attack along the lines of, 'It's all right for you, you are so confident, you have never suffered as I have suffered . . .' and so forth. Thus the troops were always deployed, but the order to fire was rarely given. Sylvia preferred a state of uneasy peace. She did not wish to hear about Frederick from her mother who had been busy trying to pass on some unwelcome news for the last few days and so she left the room again, busily pretending that she had something important to do. Yet such was her curiosity that she felt she must hear what it was that Lady Field had to say before she left, she herself would choose when and how to hear it. It was not to be pounced on her unexpectedly.

The following morning – the morning before her departure – Lady Field was helping herself to cornflakes and mumbling about the possibility of the milk being sour, when Sylvia suddenly said in the brightest of voices, 'So what's all this about Frederick? Where did you say you had seen him?'

Lady Field was a little taken aback; Sylvia had chosen her moment well. Her mother had to stop complaining about the milk, which she was enjoying doing, and change her tack altogether.

'Frederick?' she said sharply. 'What's Frederick got to do with anything?'

'I thought you had something to tell me about him?' Sylvia kept her back turned to her mother as she pretended to be dusting the windowsill. Really she was staring out of the window at the thick, black laurels and wishing that Wilf would appear like some fairy-tale prince, cutting himself a path through the undergrowth. She laughed suddenly at her own childishness and remembered similar dreams she had once had about Frederick. God! What had happened to Frederick now?

'So what's so funny?' Lady Field wanted to know. She was playing for time.

Sylvia was deeply shocked when she eventually heard exactly what it was that her mother wanted to tell her and her heart bled at the description of Frederick's physical appearance. She couldn't imagine quite how his situation might have been different, but she found the knowledge of the reality of how far he had sunk profoundly disturbing. She wanted to cry, but not in front of her mother. Where, she wanted to know, was he now? And how had Lady Field allowed him to disappear into the crowd without finding out more about him? But of course she knew that under the circumstances neither Frederick nor her mother would have dreamed of addressing the other.

Suddenly Lady Field sensed her daughter's very real distress and a twinge of compassion stirred in the depths of her consciousness. 'You're better off without him,' she said brusquely. 'Don't think about him, he gave you a dreadful time.'

'I know,' Sylvia sighed, and in a flash she saw, parading before her mind's eye, all the parishioners of old, smiling and praying and doffing their hats and saying good-morning and taking the collection and reading the lesson and embroidering hassocks and arranging flowers and nodding off in the sermon. Which of those nodding, praying, embroidering, smiling villains had noticed that the parson was always drunk and that the content of the garbled, incoherent sermons was generally Marxist? Surely none of them was clever enough for the latter. For a long time Sylvia had hoped that no one would be awake enough to realise what was really going on, but someone – or a group of people – had been and Frederick was reported to the rural dean and then the bishop had been involved and Frederick had lied and been drunk and in debt and had tried to borrow money from the lady of the manor and the whole colossal nightmare had seemed to go on and on and on, until finally Frederick had been relieved of his living and Sylvia had left him. She hated to think about those days, about the humiliation and the misery and about the awful, patronising sympathy with which she had been treated by the sneaking parishioners. Why did it have to come to the surface again now?

'Don't you worry about it all,' said Lady Field almost

kindly. 'I've told Evidence about it. If there's anything to be done, let those children look after their father.' Suddenly she was her old self again, 'They're a thoroughly selfish pair,' she said. 'Not that that's at all surprising, the way you've spoiled them.'

The next day Lady Field went home to Manchester. As the train moved out of the station Sylvia waved goodbye with an enormous feeling of liberation, almost as though winter had suddenly given way to spring, but as she turned to leave the station an immense weariness began to come over her, for what, she wondered, was she going back to? Could she really not rebuild the bridges between herself and Wilf? She realised that he had been appallingly insulted in her house because of his friendship with her, which must have made coming to see her again almost impossible, but she also feared that in some way she bore part of the responsibility for those insults. So Wilf must see her as tarred with the same brush of self-satisfied, middle-class snobbery as her mother and the Hardcastles were.

She drove slowly home, stopping only at the butcher's shop to buy a bone for Prophecy who was lounging nonchalantly all over the back seat of her car. She was feeling so restless that she didn't know what to do with herself when she reached home, or how to do anything; she didn't know whether to stand up or to sit down. She picked up the iron and filled it with water and put it back in the wrong place; she opened the fridge and looked inside without seeing anything; she sat down to read the paper she had bought at the station, but none of the headlines seemed to make any sense; she kept looking at her watch and not registering what it said – unbearable thoughts were swirling around in her head, all begging for attention. Besides Wilf and Percy Hardcastle, there was Frederick to be thought about again now. Of course she realised that Frederick was not strictly-speaking her responsibility any more, but after all she had been married to him for twenty years; she could hardly forget about him completely, particularly when she knew him to be in such a parlous state, probably with no one to turn to.

Sylvia looked out of the window at those terrible laurels. Somewhere she knew that the sun was shining – it had been lovely at the station. Perhaps she ought to take the dog for a walk – get out of the house. Perhaps if she walked she would somehow be able to sort out her thoughts and yet the idea didn't really tempt her. That sun shining in the sky seemed to be there for the sole purpose of mocking her. She sighed and decided to have a cup of coffee before making up her mind about what to do next.

All of a sudden, as Sylvia sat drinking her coffee and turning her troubled thoughts over in her mind, there was a knock at the outside door. She was electrified, she hadn't heard anyone approach and there was only one person it could be – it had to be Wilf. She jumped up, quickly smoothed her hair, put her shoulders back, pulled in her stomach and went to the door.

She opened the door with a ridiculously happy smile on her face – a real give-away smile, but there, instead of Wilf, stood Frederick. She had to blink twice before she recognised him, but the eyes were the same, deep-set in a ravaged, once-handsome face. She wasn't sure that she liked the beard very much.

There was a long silence as they both stared at each other and then Sylvia just said, 'My God, it's you . . . you'd better come in.' She half-wondered whether to kiss him, but decided that it would be quite out of place to do so.

Frederick said nothing. He didn't really know what

to say as he felt that his appearance and the very fact of him being there said all that needed saying. He just followed her quietly into the kitchen.

'You're not drunk, I hope,' Sylvia said. 'I can't cope with any more drunks at the moment.'

'No,' said Frederick, 'I'm not. I hope you don't mind me coming to see you.'

Sylvia was so amazed that she hadn't had time to ask herself if she minded seeing Frederick or not. 'How did you know where to find me?' she wanted to know.

'Gatey told me,' said Frederick and then he began to explain how he had passed out and been taken to hospital and discovered there by Milly.

'Sit down,' said Sylvia, 'and have some coffee and don't you want something to eat? You look dreadful.'

'You look all right,' said Frederick. 'In fact you haven't changed at all.'

'Why aren't you drunk?' Sylvia asked, as she scrambled him some eggs.

'I haven't any money left,' Frederick answered. 'I've drunk it all, or spent it getting down here. I had to see you again, especially after seeing Gatey – and Milly. She's a nice girl, Milly. Evidence is a lucky boy to have found a wife like that.'

Sylvia caught herself thinking, 'You were quite lucky to find me, but look what happened next.' But she said nothing, only wondered how she had survived twenty years of it. She put a plate of eggs and bacon down in front of Frederick and noticed that as he picked up his knife and fork his hands were trembling so badly that he had difficulty in eating his food.

'I was wondering,' he said, 'if I promise you I won't drink anything, might I stay here the night?'

Sylvia looked at the grey-bearded tramp sitting at her table, chasing a piece of bacon round his plate with trembling hands and knew that in a million years she could never have refused his request, but she hated the whingeing, pleading tone in his voice.

'Of course you can,' she said and sat down beside him to talk as he finished eating.

'I've reached the end of the road, you know,' Frederick said. 'I should have jumped off a bridge long ago – or thrown myself under a train. The only reason I haven't done it, I suppose, is because I haven't got the guts. If the Good Lord, about whose existence I have serious doubts, had any wisdom or mercy, He would have allowed me to die the other day when I was in hospital. Or, better still, on that lavatory floor. That was what I was expecting. By the way,' Frederick's tone suddenly changed, 'I saw your bloody mother not long ago – in the street, in Manchester.'

'I know,' said Sylvia, 'she's been staying here. She only left this morning.'

'About time she died too, isn't it?' Frederick remarked.

'She's not that old,' said Sylvia and suddenly she noticed that she and Frederick were talking to each other as though they had only seen each other yesterday. He was sober for the moment, which obviously made things easier, but she felt comforted by the familiarity of it all, by a sense of knowing what she was doing and by the extraordinary realisation that despite all the terrible rows and upheavals of the past, Frederick was the only person she had ever known to whom she could talk with absolutely no holds barred. But at the same time, as she talked, she wondered what on earth was going to happen next. Of course Frederick could stay for a few days, so long as he didn't get hold of any drink, but what on earth would he do next? She didn't like the idea of turning him out on the streets to jump

183

off a bridge or throw himself under a train, but neither did she like the idea of his hanging around indefinitely with nothing to do and needing to be looked after like some sort of overgrown child. Besides, she might be lonely, but she had learned to value her independence, such as it was. Compared to Frederick's life, hers suddenly seemed like a bowl of cherries.

They talked for a long time and Sylvia recognised all the things in Frederick which she had once most liked, in the early days before the drinking and the rows began, but there was now a kind of distance between them which lent a note of respect to their conversations. There had certainly been very little respect left on either side when they had last seen each other. But Sylvia's heart was very heavy as she realised quite to what extent Frederick had allowed himself to deteriorate, not only physically, but mentally. He rambled on even less coherently than he had done before and kept repeating things which he had only just told her, and there was an emptiness in his eyes and a listlessness about his whole being. Frederick was just one big problem that had landed, like some awful practical joke, on her plate.

That evening Hardcastle was bringing a friend – or business acquaintance – home for supper and he had asked Sylvia to prepare him a particularly elaborate meal. It was not often that he had guests and Sylvia wanted to do well by him, she couldn't think why since she disliked him so much, but in some sort of way, even he had wormed himself into her realm of responsibility. She couldn't bear to think about his relationship with his daughter as if she did, she felt sick and somehow responsible for that, too, and guilty. Contact with him seemed to have contaminated her and in a confused way that contamination made her disgusted by him but it also made her pity him.

Sylvia was laying the table in Hardcastle's dining-room when he appeared, fussing about silver salt-cellars and candlesticks.

'We'll have some linen table-napkins,' he said. 'Do things properly for once. It's not often that we use the dining-room these days.'

Sylvia made some comment about the dinner.

'I hope it will be good,' Hardcastle said. 'It's my partner who's coming, I want him to enjoy his dinner. I'm going to retire you see,' he added by way of explanation. 'I've had enough, been at the game long enough. It's high time I bowed out.'

'Isn't this rather sudden?' Sylvia wanted to know. She was genuinely puzzled that he should be concerning himself with retiring when he had the worry of Jocelyn's wedding on his mind and when she was making such exorbitant demands on him.

'My partner will take over the firm now,' Hardcastle went on. 'He's a very good man. He'll probably run it better than I ever did.' Then he turned to Sylvia and said, in what struck her as a rather strangled voice, 'Have a drink with me Sylvia, will you please. Just this once.'

'Just a glass of wine then, please,' Sylvia replied. In fact she rather liked a drink while she was cooking and certainly felt she deserved one after the events of the day; and she wasn't going to have one next door with Frederick, who she hoped wouldn't find where she had hidden her bottle of whisky.

Hardcastle went away and came back with a glass of white wine for Sylvia and a golden beaker of whisky for himself. He stared down into his own glass, Sylvia thought, almost as if he were looking for some magical answer in a crystal ball. 'I want everything to be in order before I go,' he said. 'It wouldn't be fair to leave too great a muddle for those that come after.'

Sylvia had finished laying the table so she went back to the kitchen to attend to the cooking. Hardcastle followed behind her and sat, as was his wont, at the kitchen table to talk to her while she worked. For some reason, despite everything, she felt mildly benevolent towards him as he sat there. For one thing he wasn't yet drunk and for another it was as though the arrival of his friend or partner was having some sort of effect on him and making him behave as a vaguely civilised person should.

Hardcastle was still sober when Sylvia left despite the fact that he had already started on his second large whisky. As she left he was standing by the table opening a bottle of what he claimed was his best claret.

'Give the fellow something to remember,' he said and then the front door bell rang.

Sylvia promised to come back later to clear up. She didn't want to leave it till the morning and, besides, the evening ahead with Frederick suddenly seemed quite long and she welcomed the idea of an interruption. She wondered if Frederick would watch television.

In fact the long evening was interrupted by a telephone call from Gatey.

'Mum,' she said, 'I couldn't make up my mind whether to tell you or not, I thought it might upset you, but we've found Dad.'

'I know,' said Sylvia, 'he's here.'

Gatey couldn't believe her ears because of course what she had been going to say was that they had lost him again.

She had been in floods of tears when Milly went home that morning after work to report that Frederick had discharged himself. She immediately felt that they were back at square one and that her father would disappear into the streets again, never to be seen by any of his family and surely to die unnoticed in some gutter, or on some toilet floor. She blamed Evidence for not having gone to see him and for not having begged Frederick to come and stay with him. She even thought that Evidence ought to have provided a home for Frederick and flatly refused to see the difficulties inherent in such an arrangement.

Even Evidence had shifted slightly in his attitude, influenced, he supposed, by two soft-hearted and irrational women and when he heard that his father had disappeared again he was genuinely distressed. Slowly over the days he had been steeling himself to the inevitable moment of confrontation when Milly would bring Frederick home. When he realised that this was not to be, he was suddenly bitterly disappointed and so had to admit to himself that part of him did want to see his father again.

Gatey was excited and relieved when she heard that her father had turned up with her mother and glad to hear her mother sounding quite calm about the whole thing.

'Shall I come down and see you both?' Gatey demanded, delighted at the prospect of such a family gathering.

Sylvia wasn't particularly keen on the idea as it would mean Gatey sleeping in the sitting-room, which would be a bore, and anyway she had no idea how long Frederick would be with her. For all she knew he would be moving on in the morning. Sylvia suggested that Gatey should just wait and see what happened and ring again in a few days.

In fact Gatey was very shaken by the rediscovery of her father and since returning to London she had thought of little else. She was haunted by the memory of the prematurely aged face on the white hospital pillow and by the terrible vision of her father as a tramp, cold and lonely, roaming the streets, sleeping under bridges and on park benches, kicked by passing louts or moved on by the police. There must be some other solution for him she felt, but short of his living with Evidence and Milly, which in her heart of hearts she could see was not perfect, she could think of none. So great was Gatey's preoccupation with her father that the irritation she had already begun to feel with her fellow squatters only increased as the days went by. They seemed able to think only about themselves, she decided, and in the event she gave the long-overdue sack to her boyfriend who greeted the news with dumb disbelief. She herself felt an overwhelming sense of relief: all her friends suddenly looked dirty to her and down at heel and as if they were all going to end up like Frederick if they didn't look out.

Frederick sat watching Sylvia's television and complaining about the nonsense it was showing. It occurred to Sylvia that he looked for all the world as though he had never sat anywhere else and yet she understood that, apart from the few days he had been in hospital, he had been living rough for three years or more and hadn't been anywhere near a television set, let alone a private house. Occasionally he dozed off and Sylvia wondered, as she looked at the sunken cheeks and the drawn, colourless face, whether he was not really a very sick man.

She glanced at her watch. Frederick was dozing and she thought the time had come for her to go next door and clear up the supper.

Everything she had prepared seemed to have been eaten and the dining-room table gave the appearance of two people having dined well. Sylvia was glad, it was so depressing when she had made an effort to make something good only to discover it was pushed, untouched, to the side of the plate. She cleared the table and as she carried the things back into the kitchen she heard the low murmur of voices from the sitting-room. For once it seemed as though she worked in a perfectly normal house.

XIII

Wilf missed Sylvia so much that he found himself growing increasingly morose as the days went by. Before he met Sylvia he had imagined himself to have come to terms with his loneliness, but it was surprising just how quickly she had become part of his life and what a gap there now was without her. He did not really blame her for the horrible remarks made by her mother, although he had initially felt very angry with her for saying anything to the old bag about prison. Hardcastle he knew to be a drunk, so there was hardly any point in bothering about what he said. Jocelyn was simply a bitch. He wondered what the hell the matter was with her – perhaps it had something to do with having lost her mother at an early age.

There was absolutely no question of Wilf going back to see Sylvia while Lady Field was in residence, but as to what would happen next he simply couldn't make up his mind. Sylvia was a wonderful, good, kind woman – he was perfectly sure of that and he did not see her as resembling her mother in any way, but he felt unsure of himself when he thought about her and definitely unsure of her attitude towards him. He feared that even in Sylvia there might linger a trace of class-consciousness which would prevent her from ever regarding him as an equal – especially since she had discovered, or rather since he had been so foolish as to tell her, that he had been in prison.

Wilf wasn't sure when Lady Field was due to go back to Manchester, but if he was to call again he would definitely have to wait until the coast was clear; if she were to insult him again he felt that he might not be able to answer for his actions. He certainly didn't want to land himself in prison again after all these years for beating up an old lady. He smiled wryly to himself. Of course, whether or not Wilf decided to resume his relationship with Sylvia, he was bound to be called to the Old Rectory sooner or later by Hardcastle on some job or other. That in itself might prove a decisive factor. For the moment he kept himself to himself and spoke to no one. Perhaps he should never have had anything to do with Sylvia in the first place. He had been quite all right on his own.

In the village shop, where Wilf was waiting to pay for a packet of cigarettes, a woman was talking end-lessly to the shopkeeper. Wilf just wished she would get a move on, he hadn't all day. He was feeling resentful and bad-tempered.

'Did you see that man yesterday?' the woman asked, as the shopkeeper totted up her bill. 'He was outside in the road there when I came up for some milk. I'd run out of milk yesterday morning. He was a dirty-looking man. I'm surprised you didn't notice him out there, he was asking for the Old Rectory. I thought he wanted Mr Hardcastle but he said no, he didn't. He was looking for the housekeeper, Mrs Appleby.'

Wilf started at the name.

The woman turned to look at Wilf, whose presence she hadn't previously noticed.

'Ah, Mr Wapshott,' she said, 'you spend a lot of time up there at the Old Rectory. You'd probably know all about it?'

Wilf said he knew nothing about it at all and the woman, uninterested in his denial or in anything else he might say, went on eagerly to describe the man she had seen.

'He looked like a proper tramp,' she said enthusiastically. 'Not at all the sort of person you'd expect to be asking for Mrs Appleby – after all, she looks so respectable. This man had a long grey beard and a filthy overcoat – must have had the same one for years if you ask me, but he had ever such a posh voice. Not the kind of voice for a tramp at all.'

The woman went on to describe how she had pointed out the Old Rectory and then followed the tramp down the street and seen him turn into the drive. Now, she happened to live opposite the Old Rectory and she hadn't left her house for the rest of the day so she could swear that he never came out again. She would surely have noticed if he had, unless he'd nipped out while she was in the toilet, but she never spent very long in the toilet so she doubted that being possible. 'Now what would a man like that be doing staying with Mrs Appleby?' she finally asked triumphantly.

Wilf vaguely wondered what it was all about, but put the matter out of his mind and gave it no more thought. At last the woman had stopped talking and Wilf was able to pay for his cigarettes and go. He wanted to get on, he had a skylight to replace in the next-door village, which he wanted to get done before it turned to rain.

Sylvia woke early with a feeling that something unusual was worrying her and then she remembered that of all the extraordinary things, Frederick was in the house. He had been perfectly agreeable all day yesterday and had caused no problem beyond the one posed by the mere fact of his existence, and he hadn't found the whisky. There was no question of Sylvia allowing him to stay for more than a few days, but what would he do then; where on earth would he go? That, she supposed, was ultimately his decision. Then she turned her thoughts to Wilf, as she usually did, and wished to God that he would reappear. She somehow did not feel, after what had happened, that it was for her to go and call on him, although she kept on hoping that he did not really blame her.

Then she began to think about what had happened to make her feel so fond of Wilf – to love him, in fact. A peculiar thing to have occurred, she thought, at her time of life and some might think it rather strange that he – an insignificant workman and, as it turned out, an ex-prisoner – should be the object of her passion. She had gone over and over it all again and again in her head. She knew that outsiders might suppose that her affection for Wilf had sprung merely from loneliness. Had Robinson Crusoe fallen in love with Man Friday? She thought he probably had. Having done so, did he persuade himself of his and Man Friday's profound compatibility and did he think that they were destined to meet each other to fulfil some need in the other? Did they both really think it was all 'meant' on that desert island? Wouldn't Man Wednesday or Thursday have served Robinson Crusoe equally well and been equally delighted by whoever had been shipwrecked to keep him company? Did those two really believe in the ludicrous proposition that they were made for each other? Sylvia wasn't sure that she herself really believed in quite all that, but she refused to consider the idea that her love for Wilf had grown only from loneliness. She would not – could not – have loved just anyone who might have put in an appearance at that time – Hardcastle, for instance.

Hardcastle was the living proof of her ability to discriminate – and, she thought, to choose wisely. What did she care about Wilf's background? Nothing like that mattered to her. Look what had happened to her when she married the Oxford-educated son of a bishop. Then she remembered again, with something approaching panic, that the bishop's son in question was alseep next door, presenting her with rather a problem. She wished that when Gatey had rung the night before she had agreed to her coming straight down, it would be nice to have her there to share the whole thing with. If Gatey rang again she would certainly encourage her to come immediately.

As Sylvia climbed wearily out of bed she wished that she could be surrounded by a less complicated lot of people and that Gatey had a telephone. And what was Evidence doing about the whole thing, she wanted to know? She suddenly felt very cross with Evidence and with the way he had of concentrating on looking after himself. Of course he had always been like that, ever since he was a little boy. He had been the kind of child who never lent his things and who always had more pocket money left over than any of the others, so that sometimes his mother had felt quite ashamed of him for it. It was high time he stepped in and did something about his father – and his mother, for that matter, she thought with unusual bitterness. But what could even Evidence do? What did anyone do with a burnt-out alcoholic? Sylvia wasn't about to suggest that Frederick went to Alcoholics Anonymous. What good would that do?

She dressed slowly and as she passed Frederick's door on her way downstairs she knocked on it and called, 'I'm going down to make some breakfast now.' It struck her as rather strange that she should be knocking on the door of someone whose bed she had shared for twenty years, but something prevented her from going in, it would somehow have seemed totally inappropriate. Above all, she had a very strong desire not to look at Frederick in bed. She hated the thought of him lying there, grubbily, in the rumpled sheets.

Downstairs in the kitchen she pottered about making coffee and toast and wishing that she was making it for Wilf rather than Frederick for whom, after all, she had never expected to be making breakfast again. Or had she? Deep down there was – and she felt there always would be – something about her relationship with Frederick which could never be severed. She was not sure what that something was, but she had always been aware of it, even throughout the years of separation and she had always known that when the crunch came she would never be able to turn Frederick away. Perhaps it was just that they had gone through so much together – so much hell – and, besides, she had once loved him. With a sinking feeling as she heard his footsteps on the stairs she realised that with one tiny part of her she did still love him, since she supposed that loving a person was reflected in the way you thought about them and she had noticed that despite all the horror and anger, disappointment, frustration and pain she did still look on Frederick kindly and mind about his unhappiness.

Frederick appeared in the kitchen looking slightly less ill than he had done the day before.

'I say,' he said, 'this is really most awfully kind of you.'

'How formal you sound,' Sylvia laughed. 'I'm

pleased to see you, you know,' she added. 'Strange as it may seem. But I wish you were in better shape.' She didn't want at that moment to broach the subject of how long he thought of staying, or of what on earth he planned to do in the future, so instead she changed the subject to what he wanted for breakfast.

'Your spare bed's very comfortable, you know,' Frederick said. 'I slept better than I've slept for years.'

'That's hardly surprising,' said Sylvia, 'considering the places you've been sleeping in.' She thought, but didn't add, that he hadn't been drunk, either. Poor devil, she noticed that he had to hold his cup in both hands to stop the coffee from spilling because his hands were shaking so.

'Have some marmalade,' she said, pushing it towards him. 'I must go next door for a minute and get Mr Hardcastle his breakfast. Will you be all right?'

When Sylvia had gone Frederick slowly finished eating. He wondered how long Sylvia would let him stay, he couldn't see that he was in the way at all and he might even be company for her. The best thing would be to say nothing for a while and just wait and see what happened. She'd been talking to Gatey on the telephone about Gatey coming down to see them both, so she surely wasn't in any sort of a hurry for him to go. The only trouble as far as he could see was the drink. He really didn't know how long he could hold out, or indeed whether he could ever rid himself of this terrible bugbear. It was nice being here and Sylvia was kind. In fact, Sylvia was the kindest person he had ever known. It was a pity she had left him, things might have been so different. He supposed he should never have gone into the Church and yet at the time it seemed to be the only thing he could have done. Then he had been so enthusiastic. He had been enthusiastic since about so

196

many things, but all his enthusiasms had come to nothing; now he was past all that and what was left? What indeed? Sometimes he felt afraid and as now he felt a twinge of fear he determined to put all these sickening thoughts out of his mind.

He got up and without it even entering his head that he might clear away his breakfast, he went into the sitting-room and turned on the television. That would help him not to think. Years ago he'd loved thinking, but now he had done too much of it, his thoughts seemed hard to untangle and anyway they didn't seem to lead anywhere.

Sylvia found as she went to prepare Hardcastle's breakfast that her mood had changed and she was feeling unusually cheerful. Things, she thought, could really have been a good deal worse and Frederick could have been drunk. She hoped that Hardcastle had enjoyed his supper the night before as she had put quite a lot of effort into it and it should have been good. So she moved around the kitchen with a light heart, grinding coffee and slicing bread and quietly singing an old song to herself. In her present mood she could easily believe that Wilf would soon turn up again – he was probably only waiting to be sure that her mother was out of the way – and then that awful misunderstanding would be cleared up.

'"In the same and sweet old way, I fall in love again as I did then,"' she sang. Then, 'Something, something, something ". . . as I did then,"' she went.

There was still no sign of Hardcastle by the time Sylvia had laid the table and made the coffee and toast, but she didn't want to start frying eggs until he turned up so she picked up a copy of yesterday's *Times* which was lying folded on the dresser and sat down to read it. She sat for several minutes turning the pages of the

paper when her eye suddenly alighted on the engage-
ments column on the court page. So there it was, for all
to see. The engagement was announced between Vis-
count Whatnot and Jocelyn, only daughter of Mr and
the late Mrs Percy Hardcastle . . . 'Well I never!' Sylvia
said aloud. It would all be very interesting.

She glanced at her watch. Hardcastle would surely be
down in a minute, but meanwhile she might as well go
and tidy up the sitting-room, open the curtains and
sweep the hearth.

As she walked into the hall she was singing again
gently, ' "In the same and sweet old way . . ." ' but she
stopped suddenly, for no reason that she knew, except
that all at once she was struck by an icy dread. She had
not yet seen anything to disturb her, but it was as
though something in the atmosphere itself was trying
to warn her . . . and then she saw the body – that great
body hanging there from the banisters, suspended in
the stair well with livid face and bulging, accusing
eyes . . .

She stood still for a moment and then her legs gave
way beneath her. She fell to her knees below the body,
her head swimming and her stomach heaving. She
never knew quite how long it was that she stayed there
retching before being able to drag herself back to her
side of the house and call on the only help available,
which was Frederick.

The rest of the day passed in a dream, a terrible
unending dream. It seemed like an eternity before the
doctor came and then the police and Jocelyn had to be
contacted and the solicitor who had come to supper the
night before, and it again seemed like forever before
they cut the body down and took it out of the house.
As it left on a stretcher, its monstrosity disguised by
plastic sheeting, Sylvia felt a lump in her throat and a

line of poetry – something about decay – hovered somewhere just out of reach. Something she had learned from Frederick, no doubt. And there beside her as the men struggled down the front steps with their cumbersome burden, was Frederick, head bowed in solemn respect, and Sylvia, out of the corner of her eye, saw him make the sign of the cross and heard him mutter, 'May the souls of the faithful departed rest in peace.'

When everyone had gone and Sylvia was left alone again with Frederick an eerie atmosphere of timelessness descended on the house and Sylvia and Frederick sat side by side on the sofa in her sitting-room doing nothing, saying nothing, each immersed in thoughts of death. Jocelyn had not yet arrived. It had taken some time to contact her and when she had finally been reached Hardcastle's partner had given her the news over the telephone, which Sylvia thought must have been a bad thing, but there seemed to be no alternative. Luckily she had not been on her own but with her young man, who would drive her straight down.

'I'm glad you're here,' Sylvia suddenly said, and she put her hand out to hold Frederick's skinny one. 'It would have been horrible alone.'

It seemed to Frederick that his position had been consolidated, but he wished to God he could get his hands on a drink. 'Don't you keep any drink in the house?' he wanted to know.

'No,' Sylvia said firmly, and withdrew her hand.

'Just one little one wouldn't do any harm,' Frederick said. 'After a day like today it would be medicinal, I would have thought.'

Sylvia wondered just how many medicinal drinks Frederick had had in all these years.

'No,' she said again.

'You could probably do with one yourself,' he said.

'Don't you think there must be some next door? Surely you could help yourself to a glass of whisky.'

Sylvia hadn't thought of that but the idea of Frederick creeping through to that dead house to steal a dead man's drink made her feel quite sick.

'One drink, Frederick,' she said, 'and you're out. I've got enough to put up with without that.' For all she knew she would be out herself as soon as Jocelyn arrived.

Frederick realised that for the moment he was stumped and then, as the wave of yearning died away, he thought that perhaps after all he could do without it.

Some while later, just as night was falling, Jocelyn appeared with her young man. Sylvia felt desperately sorry for her. She looked completely stunned and seemed almost incapable of taking in what anyone said or what was happening. Sylvia imagined how awful it would be to spend the night in that house, but she had lit the fire and turned the lights on to try to make it a little more welcoming. Jocelyn kept saying that she wanted to go and say goodbye to her father, but Sylvia advised her to think about it overnight; she really had no idea what words she could use to comfort the wretched girl and wondered if there weren't some aunt or friend who could come and stay with her for a few days. There seemed to be no one except the young lord and he didn't look capable of doing anything that required any more energy than smoking a cigarette. He stood there with one in his hand, tall, limp and good-looking. He addressed Sylvia with languid good manners and the tired, assured air of one who is convinced that breeding is of paramount importance.

Sylvia was of course worried about her own future. She wondered how long she would be able to stay and where on earth she would go next, but this was hardly the moment to broach such a subject and she merely asked Jocelyn if there was anything she could do for her.

'No thanks,' Jocelyn looked at her blankly, and then added grandly, 'By the way, I'd like you to stay on for a while until I've decided what I'm doing.' Jocelyn's horror at what had happened left no room for her former dislike of Sylvia, whom she now saw merely in terms of usefulness to herself.

Sylvia retired thankfully to her side of the house and to Frederick.

'Let's have some supper and an early night,' Sylvia suggested. 'Tomorrow, thank God, is another day.' But the night would somehow have to be got through and she was sure that this one and many more to follow would be haunted by the vision of that great body hanging in the stair well and by the echoed phrases spoken when she had last seen Hardcastle, only a few hours before he died. Hadn't he said, 'I want everything to be in order before I go' and something about it being high time he bowed out? Tears pricked Sylvia's eyes. There was no doubt at all in her mind now that he had not been referring then, as she thought, to his retirement, but that the whole evening had been carefully planned – down to the linen table-napkins. She felt horribly guilty.

She and Frederick sat down to sausages and tomatoes, but neither of them felt like eating – he, she supposed, because he was suffering from alcohol withdrawal, but perhaps that was unfair. In the end they both pushed their food to one side and Prophecy ended up having the sausages. The tomatoes were thrown in the bin.

'You go on up first and use the bathroom,' she said. During his years on the road Frederick had clearly lost the habit of washing and Sylvia wished that if he was going to be around for a while he might smell a little sweeter. 'Have a bath,' she said sharply.

Frederick couldn't remember when he had last had a bath. He'd had a blanket bath in hospital and a wash, but not a proper bath, although they'd been threatening him with one. Perhaps he'd discharged himself too soon. Suddenly the idea seemed rather appealing and as he climbed the stairs he thought how fortuitous it was for both him and Sylvia that he had turned up just when he had.

Sylvia sighed as she watched him go. 'Good-night,' she said and wondered what more surprises life might have in store. None for the moment, she hoped.

Just then the telephone rang. It wasn't very late but Sylvia was so tired she didn't want to speak to anyone and had half a mind to let it ring. But she could never leave the telephone unanswered in case it was one of her children who needed her.

'Wilf here,' a familiar voice said as she picked up the receiver. 'I just heard what happened and was worried about you. Are you alone?' In the horror of what had happened, he had swallowed his pride.

'Yes – no – I mean I am, but I'm not. My husband's here. . .' That sounded idiotic. 'I mean Frederick, he just turned up yesterday out of the blue.'

Wilf remembered the woman in the village shop and her description of an old tramp asking for Sylvia. Could the old tramp with a dirty coat be one and the same as Sylvia's parson husband? he wondered.

'If you'd been alone I'd have offered to come round,' he said.

'Well do, well don't,' said Sylvia. She was touched and tired and confused and relieved and couldn't think how she was going to explain Frederick to Wilf or what on earth Wilf was going to think about Frederick.

'A terrible thing to have happened,' said Wilf. 'You must be tired. I'll come round in the morning, if that's all right by you.'

'Oh do,' said Sylvia thankfully.

XIV

Six weeks later, when the sun was shining and the roses were in bloom, Jocelyn was married. She threw an enormous party with a marquee on the lawn and fireworks, and her dress which came from one of the most fashionable designers in London was made of silk especially imported from France, and there were eight bridesmaids dressed as shepherdesses with honey-suckle in their hair and five little pages looking like highwaymen in breeches and jabots and tricorn hats. Four hundred people came and the champagne flowed and there were strawberries and salmon and gardenias and hothouse lilies and, as Jocelyn remarked, all the usual things. The scent of flowers filled the church where only so recently an oddly assorted handful of people had attended Hardcastle's funeral, and a special organist came from one end of the country and a special choir came from another and the music was triumphant and the bride, of course, more beautiful than ever.

'My father would have wanted it to go on just the same,' Jocelyn said, but really she was very angry indeed with her father. He had cheated her and let her down again and she would seek her revenge beyond even the grave.

Sylvia was appalled by what she saw. She tried over the weeks to befriend Jocelyn for whom she felt only pity but Jocelyn, whilst always remaining polite with Sylvia, rejected any overtures.

As for the young bridegroom, he appeared to be totally devoid of personality or character of any kind, but he seemed besotted with Jocelyn and was obedient to her every whim. The two of them had immediately settled into the Old Rectory and even before the funeral was over had begun to talk about arrangements for the wedding. They filled the house weekend after weekend with bright – or not so bright – young things from London and a slightly decadent atmosphere prevailed.

Although Sylvia felt sorry for Jocelyn, she was also doubtful about how everything would turn out and she did not relish the thought of remaining where she was forever as Jocelyn's housekeeper. But she needed time.

Frederick, who was still with Sylvia, felt that he had entered a new phase of his life. To celebrate the fact, and to keep in with Sylvia, he had shaved off his beard, but even better than that he hadn't had a drink since arriving. Well, that wasn't strictly true as he had been completely drunk at Hardcastle's funeral and then again at the wedding. On both occasions Sylvia decided to overlook the matter as she had foreseen what would happen, there being absolutely no way of keeping Frederick away from the drink on either day. She argued with herself that Frederick's alcoholism was no longer any business of hers and as he was behaving so well the rest of the time she couldn't find it in her heart to turn him out.

In fact there had been a third incident when Frederick

disappeared to Hastings, where he now collected his social security. He didn't come back until the following day, when he appeared looking very much the worse for wear and telling a lot of contradictory stories about getting lost and clocks being wrong and about forgetting what time the last bus left. In fact, as Sylvia well knew, he had been sitting in a pub drinking his money away and had then, as he had done so often before, slept rough. But somewhere in his heart, without mentioning it even to Sylvia, he had a desire to win through this time, for there still existed in the depths of his consciousness a last scintilla of hope without which he realised he would have gone the same way as Hardcastle.

Hardcastle's death, occurring as it did so dramatically and so immediately after his arrival, affected Frederick profoundly. He felt he knew what it was to have descended to those depths of despair, for he had been there too. There but for the grace of God had he indeed gone, he thought, as they cut Hardcastle's body down from the stair well. It had never really occurred to him until that moment that in fact it was never ever too late – not until you were hanging like that from the banisters – and at that moment Frederick knew that he would rather be a drunken failure of a parson, who had made a mess of everything he had ever touched, than a bloated body on the end of a rope. About the afterlife he had ceased to think.

Because of this, and after the Hastings episode, he happily agreed to allow Sylvia to drive him to collect his social security and to wait for him outside the office until he returned straight to the car. Sylvia was surprised by his docility, but put it down to the fact that years of living rough must have knocked the stuffing out of him and, besides, she supposed that he was probably afraid of her turning him out, not that he ever mentioned the subject, or the future. Poor Frederick was not the man Sylvia had once known – years of alcoholism had blunted the sharp edge of his brain, diminished his wit and stifled his verve. She did not know what would happen to him now, but supposed that as her days in the Old Rectory were numbered she might as well let him stay until she left. He wasn't doing any harm, in fact he could be quite useful at times, busying himself with helpful little jobs about the place. She was touched and sometimes irritated by the pathetic, hangdog look he had about him when he thought he had been helpful, like Prophecy waiting to be patted, but she was delighted when she saw that the beard had gone.

Gatey came to stay and Jocelyn, most unexpectedly, offered her a room in the main house when she discovered her sleeping on the sofa in Sylvia's sitting-room. Gatey was amazed by Jocelyn and her friends, she had never seen anything like them: out of their minds on crack from morning to night, bitter, resentful and lazy. Where, she asked her mother, did they think they were going?

Sylvia had no idea, she just hated what was happening, hoped that Gatey was exaggerating and knew that sooner, rather than later, she must make a move.

Gatey was childishly thrilled by the fact of her parents being together again, if only, as Sylvia assured her was the case, for an interim period, and gladdened by the change in her father who had put on weight and even looked quite well.

'You look like you did in the old days, Dad,' she said.

Frederick looked hangdog and pleased with himself.

Since finding him in Manchester she had taken the

cause of down-and-outs really to heart so that now she worked three days a week voluntarily making tea in a drop-in centre in North London. It gave shape to her days and, she felt, meaning to her life. She even began to preach to her fellow squatters about the dangers of hanging about all day with nothing to do but smoke dope. 'Your way of life could eat into your souls,' she told them, reminding herself of no one so much as her father in the old days. Her friends couldn't see that her way of life had changed all that much so they rolled another joint and told her that they were fed up with hearing about her father although it had been quite interesting to begin with.

But Gatey was fired with so much new enthusiasm to change the world that even her mother was reminded of the old Frederick. She just hoped Gatey would be more successful.

When Lady Field heard about Hardcastle's death she was infuriated, as it clearly put her and her ominous tales of Frederick right out of the limelight. She told her neighbour that she really couldn't understand why her daughter was so upset. Hardcastle was a perfectly horrid man with absolutely no manners and, as far as Lady Field could see, he was welcome to top himself if that was the way he felt. His daughter didn't seem to like him very much so she didn't suppose he'd be badly missed.

Milly came to see her grandmother-in-law and heard a great deal more about how ridiculous it was of Sylvia to be so worked up about that awful man hanging himself. After all it was nothing to do with Sylvia. She would do better to think about her mother.

'But,' Milly suggested, 'I suppose she'll have to leave. That must worry her. What will she do?'

Lady Field was quite surprised. It simply hadn't entered her head to ask herself what would happen to Sylvia, nor had she even realised that Hardcastle's death would affect her daughter in any way, but suddenly she saw the whole drama as being to her own advantage.

'Well, now that I'm beginning to be too old to live alone,' she announced, 'she might consider coming here and settling down with me. I'd have thought she would have wanted to look after her own mother,' she paused, 'after all I've done for her.' Lady Field had forgotten that only a little while before she had been planning for Gatey to come and look after her.

'How would she earn a living?' Milly said.

'She wouldn't need much if she lived here. She could go out and get herself a little job,' Lady Field said grandly.

Milly knew perfectly well that Sylvia would rather go on the streets herself than live with her mother, but of course she said nothing. She also knew that Frederick was living with Sylvia at the moment, but she had been sworn to secrecy about that where Lady Field was concerned.

'One thing that might keep her away from Manchester,' Lady Field opined, 'might be the knowledge that Frederick is somewhere around. I had to tell her I'd seen him,' she said proudly.

Milly didn't think she would be breaking any confidences by saying that she had come across Frederick in hospital and he'd been there for several days before discharging himself. 'He just left,' she said truthfully, 'without anyone knowing where he was going.'

Lady Field was thunderstruck. 'So you mean you saw him? And Gatey and Evidence know about it?' All her cards were being trumped, but she wasn't through yet.

'One good thing about her coming up here,' she said, 'would be that it would get her away from that dreadful little man she seems to be so fond of.'

'What man?' Milly couldn't help suddenly feeling genuinely curious.

'Some dreadful little man she's picked up,' said Lady Field. 'I really don't know what he's called. Walter or Wilbur or something frightful.'

Milly laughed. 'He can't be called Wilbur,' she said. 'No one's called Wilbur except a few Americans.'

'Well it doesn't matter what he's called,' Lady Field said angrily. 'He's working class and furthermore he's been to prison. You'd think Sylvia would know better. After all, she was properly brought up.'

Milly couldn't help being fascinated, but she wasn't at all sure how much of this was true. It was very difficult ever to find anything out from Lady Field because once she was sure of your attention she was determined to hang on to it, so she would never tell what she knew quickly, but spun it out – as she thought tantalisingly – for hours.

'How does she know him?' Milly asked.

'I really don't know,' Lady Field replied, 'but he's there every day and slinks in at night and stays until all hours. It's most unsuitable.'

When Milly got home she couldn't resist telling Evidence what she had heard from his grandmother about Sylvia. It was too interesting to keep to herself, but she should have known how Evidence would react.

Since Frederick's disappearance and then reappearance Evidence had done some thinking. To begin with he bitterly regretted that he hadn't taken the chance to go and visit his father in hospital and even thought at times that he had perhaps been a little mean, not that he wanted – and of this he remained certain – to develop an on-going relationship with his father. That would have been asking too much after everything that had gone before. He realised, too, that he was immensely proud of Milly with all her warm-hearted generosity and was also slightly jealous of her for being able to be that way. Everybody loved Milly. Evidence sometimes thought that nowadays even his oldest and best friends preferred Milly to him and he minded it. When Frederick turned up on Sylvia's doorstep Evidence felt that in some sort of way he had been reprieved. He had another chance to show that he was not entirely unforgiving. He was also perfectly aware that, in any case, he ought at some stage to pay his mother a visit. Now he was beginning to feel that he might really be able to summon up the courage to kill two birds with one stone and take Milly down to see them both in Sussex.

Evidence knew that Milly was quite right to keep urging him to go and see his mother who must have had a horrible shock finding that body and who had probably had a pretty nasty time since. It wasn't as though he disliked his mother, he just could not bear being with her because of all the said and unsaid things and because of the strength of her unspoken love and because of the knowledge that he was forever letting her down, precisely by not seeing her, not looking after her in any way, not even by the occasional telephone call.

So when Milly turned up with her startling piece of news about his mother having a boyfriend who was a convict called Wilbur it threw him completely and added a whole new dimension to the picture. In fact, at first he didn't believe it and thought that Milly was just being silly. Then he decided that it was Lady Field who had been inventing lies in a typical fashion, but Milly convinced him that although Lady Field might have got it a bit wrong there was probably some truth in the story.

In the end Gatey telephoned. She had just returned to London after staying with her mother and her real reason for ringing was to try to persuade Evidence to go and see Sylvia. He ought to go; she thought it was very selfish of him not to. Gatey was always outspoken.

But Evidence wanted to know about this Wilbur person.

'Wilbur?' said Gatey. 'Who the hell's he?'

'According to Granny he's Mum's new lover,' Evidence said.

'Oh, Wilf,' said Gatey. 'He's OK.'

Evidence was appalled.

Gatey thought he was a fool. What harm could Wilf do him? 'At least Wilf goes to see her which is more than you can be bothered to do,' Gatey said indignantly.

'But apparently he's been to prison,' Evidence said.

Gatey didn't know anything about that and anyway couldn't see what difference it made. He wasn't in prison now and he seemed perfectly nice. 'A bit of an oldie,' she added.

'Perhaps my grandmother invented the bit about prison out of spite,' Evidence later suggested to Milly. But it seemed unlikely as that was not really the kind of thing Lady Field would invent.

'Under the circumstances,' he announced pompously, 'I would rather not see my mother.' And there it remained. Evidence could not tolerate the idea of his mother having a lover who was not only working class, but also an ex-convict. 'She could have done better for herself,' he said grandly.

'You're being silly and rather beastly,' Milly said, but there was nothing she could do to alter his mind.

★

When Wilf came to see Sylvia on the morning after Hardcastle's death, he was so kind and matter of fact and she so very glad to see him that they immediately recovered the ease and familiarity of their former friend-ship, and without thinking they returned at once to seeing each other every day. There appeared to them both to be an inevitability about their relationship so that they both dropped their guard and it was not very long before they became lovers. Sylvia could hardly believe what had happened as she had certainly never imagined herself embarking on a romance at her time of life and there could be no doubt about it that it was a romance for them both and she was very happy, but so was Wilf. Everything had suddenly changed and they lived only in the present.

Sylvia spent a great deal of her time at Wilf's cottage, leaving Frederick to fend for himself and to watch the television. He spent endless hours watching whatever was showing and seemed perfectly content to do so. Sometimes he thought about Sylvia and Wilf and, although he couldn't say that he really objected to Wilf, he felt bitterly jealous of him and wished that things could be otherwise. Sylvia had indeed chosen some unexpected men, he mused. First himself, about whom he didn't care to think, and then this nonentity of a little workman. He thought it was a bit of a shame really, but he kept his counsel, knowing how incredibly lucky he was to have been harboured so long. Still no one discussed what was going to happen next.

Despite the horrors of Jocelyn, Sylvia was so happy with the status quo that she couldn't bring herself to give her notice and then one day, just as she had feared, Wilf suggested marriage. She had no desire to think of the future or to make decisions. Wilf was a respectable man who had been happily married once before and who therefore believed that he could be again and, besides, he was old-fashioned enough to prefer the idea of marriage to living together. But Sylvia did not really want to get married. She had done that once and rather thought that once was enough. Altogether she was terrified of the idea of living with Wilf and destroying their idyll. She imagined herself getting on his nerves in that tiny house where everything was so very ship-shape. Then, too, there was the problem of her own independence, so hard-won and which she was reluctant to sacrifice. Apart from anything else, where on earth would she be able to fnd a job? Wilf assured her that that was quite unnecessary as he had enough for two and a nice little nest egg of savings as well. But that worried her. Gone were the youthful, carefree days when she had thrown caution to the winds and jumped at what seemed immediately attractive, without a second thought. Frederick was the ever-present reminder of such folly. This time she had to think more carefully before acting, and she was in no mood for careful thinking.

She asked Wilf for time and he, quietly confident that he would win the day, happily agreed.

Jocelyn and her bridegroom didn't leave for their honeymoon directly after the weddding but flew instead a week later to the Caribbean on the first lap of a three-month round-the-world trip. Sylvia decided that she had to speak to Jocelyn before they left and give in her notice. She would, presumably, be able to stay on until the couple returned, which ought to give her plenty of time to decide what she was going to do next.

It never occurred to Jocelyn to wonder where Sylvia would go since she had no interest in her beyond her usefulness as a housekeeper, but she was perfectly happy to accept the fact that she would be leaving some time in the unspecified future. It vaguely crossed her mind to wonder what would happen to Frederick, but she really didn't care so she didn't bother to ask. Instead she told Sylvia about her trip, how much it was going to cost and how much she deserved it after all she had been through.

Sylvia wondered if anything would ever have the power to change this strange, cold girl who had reacted so peculiarly and so distantly to her father's death. She felt certain that she herself had been more profoundly moved by it than Jocelyn had and she knew that to some extent she would carry a share of guilt for what had happened with her to the grave.

The day before she was about to leave, Jocelyn came across Frederick usefully dead-heading some roses out-side the sitting-room window. She glanced at him coldly – he was an odd fellow, but must have been quite good-looking in his time. In fact he was still, in his decrepitude, good-looking enough for her to put her head on one side, her hand on her hip, her weight on one leg and to thrust the lower part of her body forward before speaking to him.

'Frederick,' she said languidly, 'we won't be spending much time here after we get back from our trip.' She ran her free hand through her curls. 'Just the odd weekend. But we won't want the house to be left empty. I wondered if you would like to stay on as caretaker after Sylvia goes?' It struck her that she had had a sudden brainwave which, if Frederick accepted the proposition, would save her an awful lot of trouble. In fact the whole idea suited her rather well as she had never particularly liked Sylvia who still seemed to be carrying on with Wilf Wapshott down the road. Jocelyn took rather a dim view of that since it meant that the man was always hanging around the house, which she didn't want. Anyway she didn't trust him. What on earth was Sylvia doing with a man like that? But Frederick she quite liked. At least she didn't mind him. He was an odd sort of a fellow, but there was something a bit intriguing about him in a way.

Frederick could hardly believe his luck. He saw himself in a comfortable billet for the rest of his life – retrieved from the gutter by an angel. He began to wonder what Sylvia would feel about it and fondly imagined that she, seeing him rehabilitated, would turn from Wilf and come back to him. They would live as a married couple once again and he would grow roses or breed canaries and write poetry. There was no good poetry being written these days, so far as he knew. What he did not take into account was that Sylvia might feel faintly annoyed at her job being taken over by him.

In fact Sylvia thought the whole plan was utterly ridiculous. She saw Frederick living alone in the Old Rectory for months on end, with nothing to do but to return to the bottle and to all his old, wild, despairing dreaming. She supposed he might plant a couple of rose bushes in some unsuitable corner of the garden and forget to prune or spray them, but she very much doubted that he would invest in so much as one canary. As for the poetry – she couldn't even bear to think about that. But then none of it was any of her business any more.

In the years to come Sylvia often wondered exactly what it was that finally precipitated her move. Jocelyn's ludicrous offer to Frederick certainly played a part. She saw it, in fact, rather as a final dismissal. The idea of staying on in the Old Rectory as Frederick's guest was quite intolerable to her.

'Don't hurry away,' he'd said grandly. 'You have

been very good to me and I don't want to turn you out now.'

Sylvia was perfectly furious, but she knew that in his heart Frederick did not wish her to go at all. Awareness of this made her feel unbearably claustrophobic and no doubt hastened the day of her departure. But there was more to it than that. Her heart was bestowed elsewhere and all she could think of now was Wilf – night and day – day and night, and of her desire to be with him away from the nightmare memories of the past year and away from Frederick's cloying, demanding presence. Sylvia's love for Wilf and his for her combined to make a glorious bonanza, such as she had never hoped to find so late in life, and yet at first she hesitated to go because she imagined her idyll turning to dust – herself and Wilf trapped in that tiny cottage. And this time it would be until death did them part.

But the imperative of love was bound to win the day. Sylvia could no longer bear to be with Frederick when there, just down the road, was Wilf.

Frederick was amazed and saddened by Sylvia's decision to move out, and frightened of the future. He even begged her, with tears in his eyes, to stay, to live with him and look after him, but her heart, he observed, had turned to stone.

Wilf came in his van to collect Sylvia with her belongings and Frederick stood forlornly in the drive, waving them off. It seemed strange to Sylvia, seeing him there like that. She wanted to shut her eyes – to blot him out for ever. Instead she just smiled and waved and called through the window of the van, 'You know where I am, Frederick, if you need anything.'

Frederick turned and went back into the house. The young couple had long since left for their honeymoon and there was no one about. It felt very empty and

Frederick felt very alone. He wondered if there was any drink in Jocelyn's part of the house. Just one drink wouldn't hurt at a moment like this . . .

Sylvia stayed with Wilf and, despite the nagging presence of Frederick at the other end of the village and her own unavoidable feeling of responsibility for him, she was happy. Happier than she had ever been, perhaps. When a year later she married him at the local registry office Gatey brought her father, who was in a very parlous state and hanging on to his job at the abandoned Old Rectory by God knows what miracle. Evidence refused to come and Lady Field was not invited. She nevertheless let it be known that it was most unlikely that she would ever visit the couple as she didn't at all like what she had seen of Sussex and she certainly didn't fancy the idea of staying in a workman's cottage with a gaolbird.